Ex Líbrís

Cathy Vellis

REGINA

Regina

CLARE DARCY

Walker and Company
New York

CHAPTER

1

The post-chaise, having halted at the lodge to allow the great iron gates to be opened and its passenger to receive a warm greeting from the elderly lodge-keeper, bowled on briskly up the curving drive that ran for almost a mile between the silvery trunks of enormous beech trees. At last it rounded a final curve to reveal the splendid Palladian house, its wide facade—a high central block linked to wings on each side by semicircular demi-lunes—glittering silver-grey now in the flying shower that dampened, but could not darken, the pale Wicklow stone of which it was built.

As Regina Audwyn mounted the steps to the door, the sun gleamed out suddenly from between the racing clouds. An omen for good, she could only hope, for the pair of letters responsible for bringing her to Bellacourt House on this April day—a brief and enigmatic one from her uncle, the Earl of Arun, and a somewhat incoherent and much underlined one from his sister, Lady Emeline Calthrop—had been sufficiently ominous to have daunted anyone less familiar than was Regina with the Bellacourt ménage and its eccentricities. Two marriages, it appeared, were being planned at this moment within its walls, one involving Lady Emeline herself and the other Regina's young cousin Arabella, and as neither match had the approval of Lord Arun, scenes of domestic discord of the most distressing nature were—

if Lady Emeline was to be believed—being enacted daily behind that pale, serene facade.

Fortunately for Regina, she had a long acquaintance with her uncle, with Lady Emeline, and with her various young Stacpoole cousins and was therefore entirely prepared to find a crisis of some sort brewing when she came to Bellacourt House. On one occasion—this had been a dozen years before, when her mother, Lady Arun's sister, and Lady Arun herself had both still been alive—she and her mother had arrived to find the Countess's trunks being loaded into a travelling-chariot for what that lady had declared to be her final departure from a house made odious to her by the occasional presence within its walls of her husband the Earl, who, though celebrated as a traveller to exotic corners of the world, was accustomed to spend his time while in Ireland in the bosom of his family, usually creating domestic chaos there on a lavish scale. There had been a grand scene in which the entire cast of characters had enthusiastically participated: the Countess had stormed; Arabella, then aged five, had wept; the Earl had uttered *dégagé* impertinences; and Colin, only four and in the position of being all but torn in two, like Solomon's baby, by the rival claims of his mother and father to keep physical possession of him, had howled to shake the marble busts of his ancestors, disguised as Roman emperors, in their niches in the entrance hall.

And of course, Regina thought, smiling reminiscently as she trod up the steps to the handsome portico, it had ended in their all sitting down together to an excellent dinner, with the exception of Bella and Colin, who had been haled off to the nursery by their scandalised nannie, and some nine months later, while the Earl was in Afghanistan, Lady Maria Stacpoole, a robust infant, weighing all of nine pounds, had made her appearance in the world.

A few years later, after the Countess had died in childbirth, leaving the Honourable Giles Stacpoole as the final pledge of what Regina—with the experience of her present three-and-twenty years—judged to have been her genuine affection for her husband, it had been Lord Arun's widowed sister, Lady Emeline, who had provided the high drama at the moment of

Regina's arrival at Bellacourt. Lady Emeline, a true Stacpoole, with greater boldness in her strategy than her late sister-in-law, had not threatened to shake the dust of Bellacourt from her shoes in order to bring her brother to a sense of the error of his ways. Instead, she had introduced beneath its roof, on what she sweetly informed Lord Arun was to be an indefinite visit, an aged, very deaf, and very imperious female relation, who had known them both when they were in short-coats, addressed Lord Arun as—"You, boy!"—when she desired his attention, and habitually contradicted everything he said.

Within a week the inevitable explosion occurred. This time when Regina and her mama arrived at Bellacourt it was the Earl's trunks that were being removed; the elderly relation, believing him to be deserting his children forever, was having a fit of the vapours which did not prevent her from roundly abusing everyone in sight; Lady Emeline was preening herself elegantly on her victory; and in the midst of it all Colin was carried in by the head game-keeper, having fallen quite illegally from the top of the obelisk erected by Lord Arun's grandfather as a memorial to his favourite Arab stallion and broken his arm.

"My poor Julia! What a really *dreadful* way to greet you!" Lady Emeline had said, floating in her blue draperies across the black-and-white lozenges of the marble floor to place a feather-kiss upon Regina's mama's cheek.

And now, as Regina—the door having been opened to her by Hughes, the butler—passed under the corniced doorway into the great entrance hall, there was Lady Emeline coming to greet her with almost the same words upon her lips: "My poor *dearest* Reggie! What a *dreadful* thing to drag you all this way! But I felt I *must!*" She kissed Regina and cast an approving glance at the fashionable simplicity of her bronze-green redingote, which set off her slender figure to perfection. "How you manage," she said, "on the dreary pittance Etienne left you, to dress so elegantly I shall never know! All this is Paris, I suppose?"

"Yes, but dagger-cheap, really," Regina said apologetically. "You see, I found a very clever seamstress—"

"You must give me her name and direction," Lady Emeline said firmly. "Cecil shall positively take me to Paris the moment he can contrive it. I shall insist!" She saw the expression of faint puzzlement upon Regina's face and added, "I *did* write you about Cecil, didn't I? But I *must* have!"

"Oh—*Cecil!*" said Regina. "Yes. Of course. You mean Captain Barr-Walmsley, the man you are going to marry. I *don't* think you mentioned his Christian name."

She walked into the Yellow Saloon beside Lady Emeline, her movements, as always, appearing as gracefully inevitable as those of a falling leaf.

"Reggie Audwyn," one of London's fashionable young matrons had once dissatisfiedly described her, "is far too thin; she has a figure like a boy's—and the manners of one as well, when it suits her—yet she has a cool elegance that makes the rest of us appear like dowds; her smile is delightful, as every man she meets appears to discover; and I know at least half a dozen of them who would have been willing to throw the handkerchief to her since she came out of mourning for Etienne Audwyn, if only she had shown the faintest inclination to take them seriously."

To which her older and wiser mama had replied that it was not surprising that Regina Audwyn, having endured one brief experience with an unsatisfactory marriage, was unwilling, after little more than two years of widowhood, to venture into what might turn out to be a second. But this did not prevent that young lady's friends from marrying her off, speculatively speaking, to every eligible male she met both in England and on the Continent, where she had spent the greater part of her time since her husband's death.

The Yellow Saloon into which Lady Emeline now led her was Lady Emeline's own particular domain in Bellacourt House and a triumph of the art of an early eighteenth-century Italian stuccodore, who had strewn rococo scrollwork, animals, butterflies, and birds with uninhibited opulence over the ceiling and about the doorways. It was furnished entirely in the French style, with no hint of the monumental Kilkenny marble mantels and fantastically carved furniture of the black native bog oak that Lord Arun insisted upon retaining throughout much of the rest of the house. Lady Emeline, settling herself on an Empire *canapé* covered in yellow satin, invited Regina to sit beside her.

"Unless," she suggested, "you had rather go to your room at once?"

But this was so palpably a mere sop to her responsibilities as a hostess, when she was actually longing for an immediate and lengthy cose, that Regina smiled, took off her bonnet, and, tossing it upon a table, sat down beside her.

"Of course we shall talk first," she said, leaning her head, with its dark-chestnut curls, comfortably against the high back of the *canapé*. "Tell me everything at once! Are you really to marry your Cecil, and Bella her Lord Wrexam?"

"Myself—yes!" said Lady Emeline promptly. "My dear—the only man for whom I have conceived a *tendre* since poor John died! Of course I shall marry him, let your uncle say what he will—and he is making himself most decidedly unpleasant about the whole affair, I assure you! He appears to have taken the quite gothic notion into his head that because I have been a widow for a dozen years, I am therefore never to marry again!" She paused, complacently raising a hand to her still-golden hair, dressed in a most becoming Sappho. "After all, I am only nine-and-thirty. Cecil, who, as Ned will undoubtedly make a point of telling you, is a wee bit younger, considers me a mere girl still!"

"He sounds quite delightful," said Regina. "Have I ever met him? I daresay not. He must have been a great deal in the Peninsula when I was in London."

"Yes—on the dear Duke's staff. And wounded last year at Waterloo; he is only now finally quite recovered. But he is returning to active service, and we are to leave at once for Gibraltar after the wedding. Which brings me, my dear, to the crux of the whole affair. Of course you know Bella was to have made her come-out in London this spring—well, I needn't go into the effort I was obliged to make to bring your uncle to agree to that, for you *know* his peculiar notions about the education of young females! If he had his way, they would be reared like positive savages, in the style that very odd Frenchman, Rousseau, recommends. Fortunately, I have always insisted that Bella and Maria have a competent governess, so that they have *some* notion of the accomplishments a well-bred female should possess, but I quite despaired of bringing Ned to the point of giving Bella a

Season in London until Wrexam appeared on the scene. Now, of course, he is only too anxious to place her in a situation where she will meet other eligible men."

Regina, who was regarding with friendly recognition one of her favourite birds among the flight recklessly scattered across the rococo ceiling, a remarkably prim-looking dove dutifully holding a swag of plasterwork flowers in its beak, enquired what it was that had induced her uncle to take Lord Wrexam in such dislike.

"I fancy I met him once or twice during my first Season," she said, "and, if I recall correctly, every mama in London was on the scramble for him for her daughter. Immensely rich, devastatingly attractive, rather abrupt manners but an outrageous amount of charm—"

Lady Emeline spread her hands in a gesture indicative of the impossibility of anyone's pretending to understand her brother.

"My dear, he says he is too *old* for her," she said. "Wrexam *is* rising thirty-five, of course, and Bella has only turned seventeen— but then you were not much older than that when you married Etienne, and *he* was—"

"Thirty-seven," Regina said.

She turned her wedding ring absently on her finger, regarding it with a quite unreadable expression upon her face. Lady Emeline, suddenly recalling the tales that had penetrated even to Bellacourt House of Etienne Audwyn's shortcomings as a husband—tales of gallantries involving opera-dancers and demireps almost before the honeymoon was over, while the very young bride, then scarcely out of the schoolroom, had been left alone in Wiltshire—felt all at once that she had said very much the wrong thing.

To her relief, the door opened at that moment and the four young Stacpooles, swarming into the room, flung themselves upon Regina with cries of welcome.

"*Darling* Reggie! We've only this minute come in; we didn't expect you so soon or we shouldn't have set foot out of doors the whole day!"

This from Lady Arabella, a vivacious little brunette, radiating health and beauty even under the handicap of a riding-dress well splashed with mud and falling hairpins. Her younger brother Colin, who appeared to have been engaging in the same sort of violent exercise but had managed to retain an air of detached elegance in spite of it (he was the one among the cousins who most resembled Regina), advanced with an air of imperturbable dignity and, somewhat hampered by the fact that the vicinity of the *canapé* was full of young Stacpooles, succeeded in kissing her hand.

"Welcome to Bellacourt, my dear," he said, with a manner that would have done credit to Mr. Brummell himself.

"Yah! St. Cyres! St. Cyres!" his younger brother Giles amiably gibed, appearing to feel that a satirical rendering of Colin's title was the proper answer to such an egregious piece of play-acting.

Colin promptly cuffed him, and Lady Maria, a sturdy eleven-year-old who considered it her chief mission in life to aid and abet young Giles in his dedicated endeavours to bring their elder brother and sister down from the heights of their assumed grown-upness, at once attempted to hurl herself into the fray. She was restrained by Regina, who found a powerful ally a moment later when Nannie Payn, hot on the trail of her charges, entered the room.

"Lady Maria! I'll thank you to remember where you are!" said Nannie, quite scandalised, relieving Regina by snatching Maria up bodily and setting her down at a safe distance from her older brother, who was grinning amicably at her. "Now that is quite enough! Is this the way we welcome visitors?" She turned to Regina, her prim, middle-aged mouth relaxing in the very slight smile she reserved for her favourites. "I'm sure I beg your pardon, Miss Regina," she said, "but they've been that excited about you coming, you can't think! Would you like me to take them away now?"

"*I* shan't go," Giles stated, with an unconvincing air of casualness, and looking at Nannie out of the corner of his eye. He was a ruddy, fair little boy, with all his sister Bella's good looks and an equal amount of insidious charm. He clasped Regina firmly around the waist and buried his face in her redingote. "Tell her I needn't, Reggie," he said.

Regina said she would do nothing of the sort, but added that if Nannie did not object she would like them all to stay for at least a short while, until she had had a chance to see them properly.

"Well, I'm sure, miss—I should say madam—if *you* like," said Nannie, indicating by the lack of chill in her tone that the suggestion had her approval.

Regina noted—not for the first time in her visits to Bellacourt—that no one apparently had any idea of consulting Lady Emeline in the matter. Ostensibly, it was Lady Emeline who had been presiding over the upbringing of her young nieces and nephews during the past nine years, but actually it was the longsuffering and indomitable Nannie Payn who, triumphantly surmounting every obstacle cast in her way by Lord Arun, had succeeded in moulding the four young charges who had passed through her hands into what she considered (when they were on their occasional best behaviour) proper young ladies and gentlemen. She took her departure, with a final admonition to Bella and Colin not to sit on the sofa in those muddy clothes, and with some ostentation they placed themselves instead on the Aubusson carpet at Regina's feet.

"It is *heaven* having you here," Bella said with conviction. "Are you really going to bring me out? Has Aunt Em told you about Alistair? Of course I don't care in the least now about going to London, except that *he* will be there—"

Giles confided helpfully to Regina, "It's Lord Wrexam she means. She's nutty upon him. She wants to marry him, only Papa says she mayn't. If she marries him, I'll be a brother-in-law."

"You'll be an abominable little bagpipe, which is exactly what you are now!" Bella said warmly. "*Will* you be quiet and let me talk to Reggie?" She looked up at Regina with the confidence of a young lady quite accustomed to arranging life so that it went exactly the way it suited her that it should. "You *will* talk to Papa—won't you, Reggie?" she demanded. "You see, he has taken this perfectly *idiotish* notion that Alistair and I will not suit, merely because there is a difference in our ages. As if that was of the slightest consequence when two people are—are *destined* for each other!"

"Destined for each other!" repeated Colin, looking acutely ill. "Good God! Will you listen to the wench!"

Regina laughed. "Well, you are quite as bad as she is," she said. "*When* did the two of you become so appallingly grown up?"

"*I* think it's disgusting," Maria put in, from her position on a footstool that she had dragged up and placed directly before Regina. She sat upon it like a rather stout and very young idol, her elbows on her knees and her chin propped on her fists.

"Not disgusting, darling," Regina said soothingly. "But perhaps a little overdone. Oh, Uncle Ned, is that you? *Do* let me get up now, Giles!"

She detached Giles, who was still clinging to her like a limpet, and went across the room to give both her hands to Lord Arun, who had just appeared in the doorway. He was a rather short, stockily built man, with a kind of deceptive geniality and a habit of speaking his mind that was so ingrained that his family had ceased to be embarrassed by it.

"How are you, m'dear?" he said, dutifully kissing his niece. "Good journey, eh? Didn't expect you so soon. Time to have a talk with you before dinner. Come along to the library."

A chorus of voices indignantly informed him that she had only just arrived and no one else had yet had the opportunity to talk to her properly.

"Talk to her at dinner," the Earl said unsympathetically. "Talk to her tomorrow. *I* want her now. Whole place goin' to the dogs— females marryin' fellers my old father wouldn't have allowed inside the front door—"

"Cecil," said Lady Emeline, her voice trembling with outraged dignity, "is a gentleman in every sense of the word," and at the same time Bella cried, "Papa, Lord Wrexam's title is as old as yours!"

"May be as old as Methuselah's, but he ain't the man for you," the Earl said adamantly. "Come along, Reggie. No use tryin' to talk with a lot of people clutterin' about."

He put his hand under her arm and led her firmly out of the room and across the hall to the library, a rather dark room done in red, to which a yellow-and-white mantel upborne by caryatids lent a somewhat lurid relief. It had been particularly in demand as the locale of Bluebeard's Castle in the early recreations of all the young Stacpooles, and Regina could still recall a highly disagreeable nightmare, upon one of her early visits to Bellacourt, in which a prominent part had been played by the carved mask of a lion decorating the apron of a side-table of blackened mahogany, its features twisted into a particularly spine-chilling grimace.

It was still there, snarling at her, she saw as she sat down and looked expectantly at her uncle. Lord Arun, however, for a moment said nothing at all to her. He was fussing dissatisfiedly with some papers upon the table, but more, she imagined, because he did not quite know how to begin upon his subject than because he expected to find anything there. After a few moments he turned to her abruptly.

"Know this feller Wrexam?" he demanded.

Regina said cautiously that she believed she had met him once or twice. "It was years ago, of course," she added.

Lord Arun glared at her. "Wants to marry Bella," he said. "Silly notion. Told him so. First place, he's twice her age."

"If he is in love with her, and she with him, Uncle Ned—" Regina ventured to suggest, even more cautiously.

The Earl grinned at her savagely. "In love with her!" he barked. "Don't talk like a greenhead, Reggie! He don't even pretend to be! Feller's been notorious for his affairs ever since he came on the town. Taken a notion now it's time to set up his nursery, and hit upon Bella. My own fault, in a way. He's visitin' in the neighbourhood, y'know—stayin' at Harestead: Dulverton is a cousin of his—and I was fool enough to tell him how I'd brought her up one mornin' when the hunt was meetin' over there. Country life, sound principles, no town nonsense, that sort of thing. And he had a look at her and was off and runnin'. He's taken the idea in his head, you see, that he'll marry a schoolroom miss and mould her into a wife to suit. Not that he couldn't do it; he's a will of his own, and plenty of sense. But it's not the sort of thing I want for Bella."

Regina looked at him rather helplessly. From the little she knew of Lord Wrexam, it seemed very possible to her that her uncle's estimate of that gentleman's reasons for marrying might be a correct one, but she could not forget Bella's glowing eyes upturned to her as she had spoken of him.

"The point is," she ventured after a moment, "is Bella in love with him?"

The Earl snorted. "Cream-pot love," he said. "Feller cuts a good figure, has easy manners, knows how to ingratiate himself with females. I've known him off and on any time these fifteen years, and he's never been without a string of silly women runnin' after him. I won't have Bella marryin' into a muddle like that. Good Lord, Reggie, *you* know what it's like. Audwyn pretty well hauled you through hell before he broke his neck out with the Quorn, didn't he?"

Regina looked fixedly at the black snarling lion mask across the room. "If you please, Uncle Ned," she said after a moment, "I would really very much rather not talk about it, you know."

"Not talk about it? Why not?" the Earl demanded. "Never does any good not to face facts. Your husband was a blackguard; no use tryin' to wrap it up in clean linen. I told your mother how it would be when she came here talkin' about marryin' you off to him. Half-French, too. A bad business." He looked at her accusingly. "And you," he said, "you were satisfied—"

"Dazzled," Regina murmured, thinking of the look in Bella's eyes.

"Schoolroom misses!" Lord Arun said peevishly. "No sense in their cocklofts! But you found out what was what soon enough when you were married to him, didn't you?" He picked up some of the papers from the table again and began sorting through them in an abstracted way. "The reason I sent for you to come over here—" he said, and looked up again momentarily with an air of slight irritability. "Had the deuce of a time findin' out your direction, too," he said. "Why don't you live in England?"

"It's cheaper abroad, Uncle Ned."

The Earl snorted again. "Your mother," he said, "must have been fit for Bedlam when she married you off to that feller. D'ye know what she said to me when I tried to tell her he'd game away every penny he could get his hands on legally and some he couldn't?"

"I suppose she said she didn't believe you," Regina said. "Poor Mama had a genius for trusting all the wrong people, I'm afraid. But about your sending for me here—Aunt Em has been dropping hints—"

"I want you to take Bella to London," the Earl said decisively. "Open the house in Cavendish Square for the Season, bring her out—that sort of thing." Regina looked doubtful. "Now don't you begin turnin' contrary on me, Reggie," Lord Arun said dangerously. "If it's expense you're worryin' about, there won't be a ha'porth of it in it for you. I'll stand the nonsense for any gowns or fal-lals you need. And, mind, everything's to be done in bang-up style. All you want to do is to keep an eye on Bella and see she don't run off to Gretna with Wrexam."

Regina raised rather startled eyes to his. "Good heavens, Uncle Ned, you don't think he actually would—?"

"Don't know what he would do or wouldn't do. He's taken the notion in his head to marry her—I know that much—and he's damn' well used to havin' things his own way." The Earl glanced at the papers in his hand with sudden disfavour and then threw them down upon the table, where they scattered and slid off to the floor. "I'm goin' to Mexico," he announced loudly. "Been plannin' it for months and now I'm off. Leave the whole thing in your hands, Reggie. You know Emeline's taken the daffish idea to marry again. Ginger-hackled feller, younger than she is, one of the tightish clever sort, it seems to me. She has a tidy fortune, you know. Well, that's her own affair. If she wants to marry him, *I* can't stop her."

"No, of course not," Regina said, and wondered as she said it if it had ever entered either Lady Emeline's or her uncle's head to consider that the former's marriage would cause a problem of serious proportions in the household. Probably not, she thought. Being Stacpooles, they were accustomed to walking through life doing exactly what they wished to do and depending with child-like faith—or was it simply hereditary ruthlessness?—on others to cope with any destruction they left in their path. After a moment, *not* being a Stacpoole and having a hereditary dislike upon her own part of leaving things in a muddle, she said rather pertinaciously, "Uncle Ned—what about the children?"

"The children? What's the matter with 'em?"

"Nothing at all, I daresay," Regina said, "except that if Aunt Em leaves Bellacourt, you must get someone else to look after them. You can't simply leave them to the servants while you go haring off to Mexico."

"Oh!" said Lord Arun. "Is that all? That's all right then. They can go to London with you and Bella."

"With me and—!"

Words failed her momentarily. Lord Arun had the grace to look slightly guilty, but at once began blustering it through. "Nothin' to it!" he assured her. "You'll have Nannie, and Miss— whatever that woman's name is; never can remember it; the governess. And I'll send Hughes over; very dependable man, Hughes." Seeing that she was still regarding him with an accusing face he went on hurriedly, "Be good for Colin to see a little of town life. He's sixteen now, you know. And they're all deuced fond of you—"

"Uncle Ned, you are outrageous!" Regina said roundly. "You know I've had no experience—I shall go stark mad trying to cope with a London town house, Bella's come-out, *and* three children!"

"Pooh-pooh!" said Lord Arun bracingly. "You underestimate yourself, m'dear. Got your head well on your shoulders—always have had. Besides, it will only be for a few months."

"A few months? And what happens then?"

Lord Arun made a vague gesture. "Dozens of unattached fe- males danglin' on the family tree," he said. "Must be some that 'ud jump at the chance of comin' to Bellacourt. We'll have 'em in and pick the best of the lot. Nothin' to it," he repeated hopefully.

"But what if anything happens in the meantime? With you in Mexico and Aunt Em at Gibraltar—"

"Give you the name of my London solicitor," Lord Arun offered. "Very competent sort of feller—used to dealin' with any- thing—"

"With Giles coming down with chicken-pox or Colin having delusions of being twenty-two and going off to the Fives-court or some low tavern in Holborn with *quite* undesirable persons? To say nothing of worst coming to worst and Wrexam persuading Bella to elope with him? Uncle Ned, have you *no* imagination?"

"Shouldn't think I had," the Earl said cheerfully. "Not much use to a feller, as far as I can see. Besides, none of those things is likely to happen." He came over and clapped her encouragingly upon the shoulder. "You'll have a splendid time in London, m'dear," he said. "See if you don't. You've been about the world enough now to be well up to snuff; not as if you were a school-room miss. And you'll meet all sorts of eligible men at the *ton*-parties; might get yourself off as well as Bella before the Season's over. Time you were marryin' again, you know."

Appearing to think he had now settled the matter, he walked over to the door, opened it, and invited her to join Lady Emeline and her young cousins again.

"Deuced fond of you, all of 'em. Always were," he repeated genially. "Tell 'em now they're to go to London with you, if you like. Put 'em in high gig—"

"Uncle Ned, I shall tell them nothing of the sort!"

"Oh? Eh? Well, just as you like, m'dear," said the Earl. "Tell 'em tomorrow; there's plenty of time. D'ye mind closin' the door as you go out? Devilish draught in here." He stooped and picked up the fallen papers from the floor. "Now where did I put—?"

Regina gave it up and departed.

CHAPTER 2

As daunting as the prospect was of assuming temporary responsibility for four remarkably lively young people, the success of a
ton debut, and a very large town house in Cavendish Square,
Regina was quite aware, from the moment she left her uncle in
the library, that it was impossible for her to escape the task. The
Earl would certainly go to Mexico; Lady Emeline would marry
her Captain and be off to Gibraltar; and short of abandoning the
younger members of the family to the care of servants until some
older female relative might be found who was willing to under-
take their upbringing, there was nothing to be done but for her
to accept the rather staggering charge that had been laid upon
her.

But at least, she thought, trying to look at it philosophically, it
would not be dull. London in the Season, with a great town
house as a setting, and the furious pace of a never-ending succession of balls, routs, breakfasts, and opera-parties as a daily rou-
tine, would most assuredly offer her a welcome change from the
genteel economies of her recent existence, and if difficulties arose
there would always be Mr. Pipping, for such, she was informed
by Lord Arun that evening, was the name of his invaluable solicitor, who was presumably prepared to cope upon demand with
everything from mumps to pertinacious peers.

She was conscious of a certain curiosity concerning the particular pertinacious peer against whose attentions it would be her

duty to guard Bella during that London Season, and, as it happened, it was a curiosity that was to be satisfied on the very morning following her arrival at Bellacourt. She had been invited at breakfast by Bella and Colin to accompany them on a morning ride, and the three of them, having set off down the beech-lined drive to the lodge gates under a pale spring-morning sky covered with thin white clouds, had just turned their horses' heads in the direction of the ruins of a mediaeval abbey visible at the top of a nearby rise—a romantic pile of violet-grey stone covered with lichen and trailing ivy—when they came in sight of another equestrian, a gentleman in a dark-green coat of impeccable cut, astride a raking grey.

"It is Lord Wrexam!" cried Bella, forgetting, it appeared, in the surprise of the moment, that she was upon Christian-name terms with her beloved. "He is coming to see me, I expect. He does, you know, though Papa dislikes it so very much."

And she spurred her mare impetuously forward, leaving Regina and Colin to follow at a more leisurely pace.

Regina, gazing critically at Lord Wrexam's tall, broad-shouldered figure, which showed to excellent advantage in riding-coat and buckskins, was obliged to admit that it was scarcely to be wondered at that Bella had conceived a violent *tendre* for him. His close-cropped black hair, sporting neckcloth, and white hunting-tops proclaimed the "top-of-the-trees" Corinthian; his dark face was handsome, with strongly marked black brows and a decided cleft in the chin; and the expression of rather autocratic boredom upon it was leavened by a distinct hint of humour about the well-cut mouth. It would be difficult, she thought, for any woman to whom he chose to pay court to remain entirely indifferent to him; a schoolroom miss like Bella must have been *bouleversée* at first sight.

As for Wrexam himself—if *he* was in love, she thought, he most assuredly did not show it. Indeed, if there was any emotion at all, other than courteous attention, in the look he bent upon Bella, it seemed akin to the incipient satisfaction of a schoolmaster gazing upon what he considers prime soil in which to plant the seeds of wisdom. Which unlikely simile—for anything less resembling a schoolmaster than the dashing figure sitting easily in his leathers astride the grey it would have been difficult to imagine—brought her sudden delightful smile to her lips as she came up with him and Bella, so that it was with an expression of quickly repressed amusement upon it that Lord Wrexam, glancing up from his conversation with Bella, first saw her face. Quite obviously he did not recognise it, which was scarcely surprising, since when he had seen it last it had belonged to a very young and coltish Miss Royd in a sadly countrified white muslin frock, instead of to an elegant young widow wearing a scarlet riding-dress in the first style of fashion and surveying him with a frank and quite composed regard. He bowed slightly in her direction as he greeted Colin, and Bella, brought back by the words from her rapt contemplation of her beloved, glanced round and said, "Oh—Reggie, you are acquainted with Lord Wrexam, are you not? Alistair, you will remember my cousin, Mrs. Audwyn."

Lord Wrexam, his black brows lifted slightly, appeared about to disclaim any previous knowledge of Mrs. Audwyn when Regina came to his assistance by remarking that she had not been Mrs. Audwyn, but Miss Royd, when they had last met.

"It was some years ago," she said. "I daresay you will not remember."

"Ah, but I rather think I do—now that I've heard you speak!" Lord Wrexam said promptly. "You are Brummell's Arethusa."

"Brummell's *what?*"

"Arethusa. Do you know your mythology, Mrs. Audwyn? She was a wood nymph who was changed into a fountain to enable her to escape the attentions of the river-god, Alpheus. Brummell said he was certain if she could have spoken she would have had your voice."

"Oh, what a pretty compliment!" cried Bella enthusiastically. "And quite true, too. Reggie *has* a lovely voice."

She looked proudly from her beloved to her cousin, with something of the air of a playwright who has just observed a very creditable performance of a scene of his composing; but Regina immediately proceeded to spoil the effect by looking quite indifferent and turning the conversation to the horse Lord Wrexam was riding. To say the truth, her first reaction to his compliment had been as agreeable as even Bella could have wished; but she had at once brought herself up sharply. If it was to be her duty to guard Bella from the attentions of Lord Wrexam, it would certainly be a poor way to begin by allowing herself to be charmed by him.

And that he intended to charm her she had not the least doubt. Bella must already have informed him of the plans that were afoot for the coming Season, and the very first thing he would therefore desire to do would be to put himself upon amicable terms with her cousin, so that she would allow him to run tame in the house in Cavendish Square while she was presiding over it.

In taking this view of Lord Wrexam's intentions, however, she was doing him something of an injustice. It was true that he most assuredly had it in mind to be a frequent visitor in Cavendish Square that spring; it was equally true that he was perfectly willing to put himself to the trouble of being agreeable to Bella's very attractive cousin in order to smooth his way towards that end.

But if Regina had the slightest notion that he considered her as an obstacle of any importance in his path, she was soon to be disabused of it. This enlightenment, indeed, burst upon her almost at once, when, after allowing the conversation to proceed for the short period she considered bare civility demanded, she sketched an adieu to Lord Wrexam and suggested to Bella and Colin that they go on with their ride.

But Lord Wrexam, who appeared to read without difficulty the challenge that was being issued to him, at once took it up.

"By all means," he said, fixing Regina with a gaze which she could only characterise as one expressive of a total disregard of her interference. "I shall accompany you, if I may."

It seemed hard to Regina that she could not say, "Oh no, you will not!"—and so bring the battle into the open; but she had been too well brought up to be uncivil even when she felt it to be richly deserved, so she merely said she was sure he would be bored, as the children were only taking her about to renew her acquaintance with places in the neighbourhood that had pleasant past remembrances for her. Bella, looking very much put out at being classed as a child, immediately said that he wouldn't be bored in the least.

"Of course I shan't be. Bored in the company of two such lovely ladies!" said Wrexam, and he looked at Regina with a smile of rather quizzical amusement in his slightly narrowed eyes.

He is daring me, she thought, *to be rude to him, and, what is more, he is quite prepared to be even ruder to me if I am;* and a slight colour came into her face.

Fortunately, a diversion was caused at that moment by the appearance upon the scene of Lord Arun, who came pelting up on a fine half-bred hack, rather, Regina could not help thinking, like young Lochinvar riding out of the West, only intent upon carrying off a daughter instead of a bride. He reined in his steed with a flourish, and addressed Wrexam in no uncertain terms.

"Hi!" he said. "What do you think *you're* doin' here?"

Wrexam, who did not appear in the least taken aback by this unceremonious greeting, remarked in amicable tones that, as they were outside the gates of Bellacourt, he had quite as much right to be where he was as had Lord Arun.

"I thought," he said, turning the subject, "you were going to Constantinople, Arun."

"Mexico!" snapped Lord Arun truculently. "And *not* before I've got Bella safe off to London, away from you!"

Regina saw Colin and Bella exchanging glances of anguish, indicative of *Papa's being the irate father again.*

"Ah, but I shall be returning to London very soon myself, you know," Wrexam remarked calmly. "You had really much better give it up, Arun. You can have no real objection—"

"Yes, I can!" Lord Arun shouted. Steadying his horse expertly with one hand, he pointed a finger of the other accusingly at Wrexam. "You're a rackety, ramshackle care-for-nobody, Wrexam!" he said. "Nothin' sober and steady about you! Lead a girl a miserable life. Ask Reggie. She's been through it. Bread-and-butter miss married to a man of the world. Result to be expected—played her false before the honeymoon was over. Won't have that happenin' to Bella!"

If Regina could have had her wish, a heavenly messenger

would have descended at that moment and removed her uncle to foreign parts before he could utter another word. She saw Wrexam glance at her curiously. Bella gave a little shriek and cried, "Papa!"—and Colin, rising magnificently to the occasion, enquired of Wrexam in a *dégagé* manner if he had made up his mind to purchase the horse he was riding.

"A little short of bone, ain't he?" he went on disparagingly, deliberately intent, it seemed, upon drawing Wrexam's attention to other matters by impugning his reputation as a judge of horseflesh.

His lordship, however, refused to be drawn. "No, I think not," he said quite good-humouredly. "Would you care to try him? I believe—"

"No, he wouldn't!" shouted Lord Arun. "We're not ridin' with you, Wrexam! You're not wanted!"

"Papa!" said Bella again, indignantly. "How can you!" She suddenly turned to Wrexam and, with her Stacpoole talent for taking the bull by the horns in the most public manner possible, said to him with great dignity, "We are having a small party this evening in honour of Reggie's arrival. Will you come?"

"Here!" exclaimed Lord Arun, his ire instantly directed to his daughter. "What's this? A party? First I've heard of it!"

"Well, Papa, of course we must do *something* about Reggie's coming to us!" Bella said, with a grown-up air. "She will think it *quite* odd if we do not."

She turned a look of appeal upon Colin, who again rose nobly in support of her.

"Only a small gathering," he said negligently to Wrexam. "Quite impromptu, one might say."

"Impromptu!" said Lord Arun explosively. "I should think it was! You're cuttin' a wheedle, both of you! You never thought of such a thing till this very moment!"

Lord Wrexam, evidently considering it an excellent idea to take his departure before the invitation could be withdrawn, promptly said he would be delighted to come and rode off—"and if the back of one's head can grin," Regina thought exasperatedly, "*his* is certainly doing it. He will most assuredly appear at Bellacourt this evening, and one can't very well show him the door! If this is a sample of what I shall be obliged to cope with in London, I think I had best tell Uncle Ned here and now that I shan't be adequate!"

It was not the moment, however, to tell Lord Arun anything. He was, it appeared, in a towering temper with his two eldest offspring, and accused them, in a breath, of rag manners, lack of respect for their elders, and the basest ingratitude, quoting King Lear to them on the latter subject with a voice and gesture that would have done credit to Edmund Kean himself. He then, as if suddenly realising that he was making himself a motley to the view and that even Regina was finding it difficult not to giggle, just as abruptly calmed down again and said matter-of-factly that if they were going to have a party that evening they had best see to getting some people in.

"What about the servants? Surely they will require some notice?" Regina suggested, to which all the Stacpooles politely agreed, but none of them seemed willing to cut short his or her ride for the purpose of bringing notification to Bellacourt of the festivities they had planned for the evening. Regina, with her previous experience of the Stacpoole ménage, was quite aware that as a result of this omission notices would fall upon Lady Emeline's head like autumn leaves, that the cook would contemplate suicide in the kitchen and harass his minions beyond endurance, that housemaids would fall out with and over one another as they scurried about doing the housekeeper's frenzied bidding, and that every groom, footman, and gardener in the Earl's employ would spend his time speeding through the countryside bearing hastily scribbled invitations, besides moving furniture, carrying up bottles from the cellar, and staggering about with enormous coal-scuttles.

But in the end, as it always happened, Bellacourt House, its long Palladian windows ablaze with candlelight in the soft April darkness as the first carriages began to rattle up the beech drive, its great front door hospitably open to receive its guests into the spacious hall, with its elegant *grisaille* roundels and marble busts of earlier Stacpooles, would stand ready to add still another evening of gaiety to those that so often had been enjoyed within its walls in the past. The truth of the matter was, she dared say, that the servants had come to expect the unexpected at Bella- court, and would have felt rather cheated if life had gone on there in the ordered, humdrum manner that it did in other houses.

CHAPTER

3

The ballroom at Bellacourt was a huge apartment built out at the rear of the house, and modelled grandly upon Palladio's concept of an Egyptian hall. There were scagliola columns, massive gilt chandeliers brought back from an Italian palace by a Stacpoole ancestor who had made the Grand Tour, a white-and-gold compartmented ceiling, and a superb parquet floor. When Regina entered it that evening, she was not surprised to find a housemaid engaged in whisking off the last of the holland covers that shrouded the chairs and sofas when the room was not in use, but she vanished into an anteroom with the speed of a conjuror's rabbit just as the first guest appeared. The small orchestra hastily hired for the dancing then immediately struck up a gay tune, quite as if they had not been hustled into the house and installed in their places only moments before.

Not to Regina's surprise, an impressive number of guests also began magically to stream into the house and fill the ballroom. Bellacourt House was famous for its hospitality, which was hardly ever of a tame and usual variety (on one occasion a renowned cantatrice, engaged for the evening, had eloped after her performance with one of the younger sons of the house, whom she had never laid eyes on before that night, and on another two gentleman guests had remained behind to fight a duel in the ballroom, leaving a bullet hole as a souvenir in one of the scagliola columns), so that no one cared to miss whatever ex-

traordinary event was about to be served up along with this unexpected evening-party.

Regina, who was well acquainted in the neighbourhood, had
the pleasure of seeing many familiar faces, and was instantly im-
portuned by several gentlemen to stand up with them for the
first set of country-dances. This was scarcely to be wondered at,
as she appeared to particular advantage that evening in a high-
waisted frock of pale orange silk—shrieking of Paris, as Lady
Emeline enviously observed—with her dark-chestnut hair twisted
into a knot on the top of her head and falling in careless ringlets
on either side of her face.

She dismissed them all, however, to bestow her hand upon
Captain Barr-Walmsley, whom Lady Emeline had seized upon
as he entered the door and brought up to present to her with the
air of one bestowing a handsome gift upon her.

"This," she said impressively, "is Cecil. Isn't he *divine?*"

Captain Barr-Walmsley, a sandy-haired man in his middle
thirties with a guardsman's moustache, blushed and bowed.

"*Quite* divine," said Regina kindly, surveying him with a
rather detached but not unfriendly regard, which caused him to
blush even more hotly, until she wondered if he might set his
collar afire.

"You are t-too k-kind, ma'am," he said, upon which Lady
Emeline said benignantly that he must call her Reggie, as he was
so soon to be in the family, and instructed him to dance with her
niece so that they might become acquainted.

"I am afraid," Regina said thoughtfully, as she and the Captain joined the set, "that she is awfully used to having her own
way. I sometimes think people must be a little mad to marry
Stacpooles, but they all seem rather to enjoy it, once they have
done it. I daresay it is because they are never bored."

Captain Barr-Walmsley said fervently that he would never,
never be bored with Lady Emeline.

"I often think I never really began to live until I met her," he
said ingenuously. "Not another woman in the world like her—
what?"

Regina said quite truthfully that as far as she knew there was
not, and was thereupon treated to a detailed history of Captain

Barr-Walmsley's courtship of Lady Emeline, which had had a sometimes stormy course, owing to Lord Arun's outspoken opposition, and of his present hopes of beginning shortly upon a life of permanent bliss with his beloved at Gibraltar.

Regina, who knew Lady Emeline very well, was quite sure that Gibraltar would serve only as a brief way-station in her journey through life and that the love-stricken Captain would very soon find himself enjoying a brilliant social life with her in Paris or London; but she did not see fit to disillusion him, and after a short while her attention was distracted by the sight of Lord Wrexam entering the room. He was one of those few fortunate men, she was obliged to admit, who looked as if he had been born to wear evening-dress, and whose figure surmounted with aplomb the difficulties posed by the fashion for wasp-waisted coats, knee-breeches, and striped silk stockings. As she watched, he strolled into the room quite as if he had not been pointedly invited by his host to stay away, was greeted enthusiastically by Lady Emeline, who always delighted in crossing her brother, and, raising his quizzing-glass to his eye, surveyed the assembly in a leisurely manner.

"Looking for Bella," Regina thought very accurately, and in a few moments she saw him making his way across the ballroom to where her young cousin, who, she suspected, was not dancing because she had been waiting for him to appear, was seated in conversation with a pair of young men.

Strictly speaking, of course, as Bella was not yet out, she should not have been attending evening-parties, but with the usual Stacpoole disregard for convention she had been doing so in her own home since she had turned sixteen, and had already wreaked a good deal of havoc among the neighbourhood swains with her piquant little face and perfectly natural and unaffected manners. This evening, in a simple white frock of Indian mull muslin, with her hair artlessly dressed à l'Anglaise, she was looking particularly charming. As Lord Wrexam approached her, he might have been pardoned for coming to the critical conclusion that it would have been difficult to discover a young lady better suited to wear a countess's coronet and to become the ancestress of future Earls of Wrexam.

Regina saw him greet her with easy address, saw the glowing, eager face her young cousin turned upon him as she impulsively jumped up and gave him both her hands—and her mind instantly ran back half a dozen years to recall an evening at Almack's, another young girl in a white muslin gown, and Etienne Audwyn's dark face smiling down at her as he had appeared unexpectedly before her and asked her to dance.

But of course she was not Bella, Regina reminded herself; she had not, and never would have, her young cousin's splendid Stacpoole insensitivity to the subtle shades of human behaviour. Perhaps Bella, who, in spite of her ingenuous air, had quite as much self-will as the rest of the family, could have obliged Etienne to include her in his life, whether he was bored with her lack of worldly experience or not; for he had been, all in all, she realised now, a rather weak man.

But Wrexam, she thought, regarding him as he stood conversing with an air of amused tolerance with Bella and her young companions, did not look in the least like a weak man. He looked, on the contrary, like a man who knew particularly well what he wanted and, in Lord Arun's words, was damned well used to having things his own way.

Under the circumstances, and knowing the readiness with which any girl of Bella's age might fall in and out of love with such a dazzling figure as Wrexam, Regina was inclined to believe that her uncle was quite right in his opinion that his daughter's chances to find happiness in life would be much improved if Wrexam could be prevented from marrying her. And she determined then and there to do her possible to see to it that Bella at least had the opportunity to meet other eligible men nearer her own age before she committed herself irretrievably to that dashing peer.

Not to her surprise, Wrexam, having stood up with Bella for the ensuing set of country-dances (much to the wrath of Lord Arun, who was prevented only by the joint efforts of Lady Emeline and Regina from causing the sort of scene that would have rewarded his guests for the trouble they had taken to attend the party), next approached Regina to solicit her hand for the waltz.

Regina, in two minds as to whether it would be better to snub
him by a refusal or seize the opportunity to make it clear to him
that her opposition to his marrying Bella would be quite as adamant as Lord Arun's, chose the latter course, and as a result soon
found herself gliding about the floor with quite the most adept
partner she had ever had.

"How well you dance, Mrs. Audwyn," she heard him remark
presently, as if in reflex to her own thoughts, when he had introduced several conventional topics of conversation and had received only the briefest of replies to each for his pains. "Arethusa, indeed—for I must say that, in addition to your being quite
as light as a spray of water, I believe even dancing with a wood
nymph who had been turned into a fountain could not possibly
be a more *damping* experience than this."

Regina, startled by this unexpected attack, was almost betrayed into a ripple of laughter, but repressed it sternly and
asked in her usual cool manner if he had expected she would be
as easy to charm as Bella had been.

"I'm not, you know," she said. "In fact, I daresay I should
warn you that you are wasting your time even to try. You see, I
quite agree with Uncle Ned that Bella is far too young to think
of fixing her affections, and nothing you can say is really at all
likely to make me change my mind about that."

Lord Wrexam, looking down at her, appeared quite unper-
turbed by this frankness upon her part.

"Really?" he said amiably. "Well, it's much better to know
one's enemies, isn't it? It makes life so very much simpler in the
long run."

"Exactly."

"You won't object if I ask you whence this sudden antipathy
to me arises?"

"Not at all. In point of fact, it isn't anything in the least personal. It's merely that Bella is so young—"

"I shouldn't beat her, you know," Wrexam said conver-
sationally. "As a matter of fact, I am really quite a mild-mannered sort of fellow."

"The sort of mild-mannered fellow," Regina said pointedly,

"who comes to other people's houses when he has been asked most particularly to stay away—"

"Ah," said her partner reasonably, "but Bella didn't ask me to stay away."

"It is *not* Bella's house. It is my uncle's."

"And Lady Emeline, too, seemed rather pleased to see me—"

"You are quibbling," Regina said severely. "Let me tell you, Lord Wrexam, that when I have Bella with me in London I shall give particular orders that you are not to be received."

"No—will you? That will be rather unwise, won't it? After all, you know what girls are—if they can't see a man they wish to see in their own homes, they always manage to slip out."

"No doubt *you*, Lord Wrexam, have had wide experience in that sort of affair!"

"I? No, I'm bound to say I haven't. I've never cared much for the infantry, you see. To my mind, women, like wine, are much more interesting when they've aged a bit."

"Then I wonder you should be so determinedly pursuing my cousin!"

"Do you, indeed? Somehow I should have thought the answer to that would have occurred to you. You seem a very intelligent girl."

Regina looked up at him quickly, moved at last out of her aloofness by his maddeningly cheerful air of complete equanimity.

"You really are *quite* insufferable, you know!" she said warmly.

Wrexam raised his brows. "Because I called you a girl? But you seem so to me, you know. You must be all of three- or four-and-twenty, I daresay—a mere child, compared to what it appears you and Arun are determined to consider *my* advanced age! By the bye, I *am* only thirty-five."

"I am not," Regina said loftily, "in the least interested in your age, Lord Wrexam. *Nor* in your opinion of mine—"

"Made it a year or two too high, I expect," said Wrexam sympathetically. "Pray accept my apologies. I didn't mean to imply that you *looked* twenty-four, but you seem so determined to make yourself out a dowager—"

Regina choked over a spurt of reluctant laughter.

"That's better," Wrexam said approvingly, whirling her expertly down the long room. "I daresay you have quite a delightful laugh, if you could only be persuaded to let one hear it. But to return to the matter we were discussing a few moments ago—you must certainly be aware of the advantages to be gained by a man in choosing a very young and unspoiled bride. Young ladies of fashion who have had a Season or two in London and have had their heads turned by their own success, until they have arrived at the settled opinion that the world revolves for their convenience, can make abominably uncomfortable wives, you know! To say nothing of devising every imaginable sort of stratagem to induce their husbands to spend half the year in town, when they would be far better occupied in the country, they usually expect the poor devils to indulge them in each fashionable whim they take it into their heads is indispensable for their comfort—"

"I see!" Regina said. "Of course love—a mutual regard, at least—has nothing to say in the matter, by your idea! One chooses a wife as one chooses a horse—the proper blood lines, good conformation, a tractable disposition—and satisfaction automatically results!"

Lord Wrexam, she saw, looked not at all nettled by her frankness, but merely remarked coolly, "If you wish to put it so baldly—yes! In my opinion, if a man chooses a wife with *less* care than he expends in selecting a horse, he may properly be set down as a nodcock. If he rides thirteen stone, for example, he will certainly—if he uses the least prudence—not buy a horse that is not up to that weight. Equally, a man who—as happens to be my case—is accustomed to leading his life as he chooses, without ever having been burdened with the necessity of bowing to the whims of a frivolous, self-willed young woman, would be guilty of the greatest folly, it seems to me, if he were to marry a wife who answers to that description. Lady Arabella on the contrary, has been bred almost entirely in the country; she enjoys country life, hasn't the slightest experience of an existence in which flirting, gaming, and shopping for expensive gewgaws are the chief amusements—"

"Lord Wrexam," Regina interrupted him, with indignant conviction, "if you were going about it to make me dislike this marriage, you could not have succeeded better! Confess—you have not the slightest regard for Bella!"

"If you mean have I formed a violent *tendre* for her—I have not."

"No—I should think it highly unlikely that you had ever formed a *tendre* for any woman!" Regina said, civility and decorum now thrown entirely to the winds. "I thought I had met cold-blooded, cynical men in the course of my life, but let me assure you, Lord Wrexam, that in this regard you bear off the palm! Has it never occurred to you that Bella deserves better than—?"

"This feller annoyin' you, Reggie?" Lord Arun's voice suddenly interrupted, at her elbow.

She looked around, startled. He had, it seemed, been dancing with a stout dowager in puce, whose placid careering about the room he had brought to an abrupt halt without the slightest apology. Regina, conscious that the obvious appearance she must have presented of quarrelling with her partner had been responsible for her uncle's lapse, flushed vividly.

"No—no, of course not," she began, rather incoherently.

"Because if he is," Lord Arun said emphatically, glaring at Wrexam, "I'll have him removed. I'm a believer myself in Irish hospitality, but when a feller's told he ain't wanted and turns up anyway—"

"Ned, you are making a fool of yourself, *quite* as usual!"

Now it was Lady Emeline, Regina saw in despair, who had stopped dancing to take a hand in the matter. Lord Arun, transferring his glare from Wrexam to his sister and her partner, Captain Barr-Walmsley, regarded them with impartial disapproval.

"Who," he enquired rudely, "asked *you* to meddle?"

"Oh, I say—look here!" Captain Barr-Walmsley expostulated, rushing to the defence of his betrothed. "Really, you know, sir—!"

Lord Arun looked at him with distaste. "Oh, go away!" he said impatiently.

"Ned, if you intend to create a scene, I warn you I shall scream!" Lady Emeline broke in feelingly.

Lord Arun snorted. "And *that's* a tottyheaded thing to say!" he remarked derisively. "Scream the house down, if you like. I want this feller out of here!"

He looked truculently at Wrexam, who said with an air of resignation, "Really, Arun, you are being extraordinarily tiresome! Your entire act is extremely *vieux jeu*, you know. This sort of thing simply isn't done any more."

"Well, I'm doin' it!" Lord Arun said incontrovertibly. "And what's more, I'll keep you away from my daughter, b'God!"

"I am sure," Wrexam said approvingly, "that sentiment does honour to your paternal feelings. But if you are really in earnest, it appears to me it will be necessary for you to postpone your journey to Mexico—"

"No, it won't!" snapped Lord Arun. "Reggie'll see that you don't try anything on—"

By this time the musicians in their gallery above were craning their necks to see what was going on and were keeping deplorable time; half the waltzers had stopped waltzing and were frankly staring, and the polite few who continued to revolve to the music were quarrelling bitterly with their partners as to which one was to have the privilege of facing the field of combat. Bella, of course, seeing what was going forward, came up, followed bashfully by her partner, a blushing youth of her own age, and, with Stacpoole virtuosity, began to weep in a very becoming manner, merely allowing several large crystal tears to overflow her eyes while she accused her father in a broken voice of wishing to destroy all her happiness.

"Don't be a ninny, girl!" Lord Arun said irritably. "It's your happiness I'm tryin' to see to." He turned suddenly and quite unexpectedly to Wrexam. "Look here!" he said. "If you had any sense in your cockloft you'd stop tryin' to marry Bella and have a touch at Reggie instead. She's been through the mill—*she'd* know how to handle a feller like you. Take it all in her stride now. She's a dashed pretty girl, too, you may have noticed. Not in her first bloom, but you can't have everything—"

"Upon that note," Wrexam said firmly, refraining manfully from looking at Regina, "I shall take my leave. I have only one parting request for Mrs. Audwyn—that, no matter what other iniquities she may lay in my dish, she do me the justice to admit that *this* idea cannot be included among them. Lady Emeline"— he bowed over her hand—"your servant. Bella, my dear—"

He took Bella's hand in his, dropped a light kiss upon it, and was gone.

"I *do* think, Papa," Bella said, indignation sparkling through her tears, "that it was perfectly *beastly* of you to say such a thing! As if Alistair would ever think of marrying anyone but me!"

Lord Arun opened his mouth to speak, but Lady Emeline, freed from Wrexam's disturbing presence, had already taken the situation in hand.

"Come along, Ned!" she said decisively. "You are going to have a glass of champagne with Cecil and me; it will make you feel ever so much better. Reggie, will you take Bella upstairs until she is calmer?"

Regina, feeling the utmost relief at the idea of escaping from the ballroom, linked her arm in her young cousin's; the musicians struck up another waltz; and the guests went on very happily with their dancing, gratified to have another Stacpoole scene to add to a list whose origins went back to a perhaps apocryphal occasion upon which an eleventh-century Gerald de Stacpoole had thrown a beaker of mead at his eldest son's head and hit William the Conqueror instead, thus causing the aforesaid Gerald to form a sudden decision to take up permanent residence in Ireland.

CHAPTER

Regina did not remain at Bellacourt for the wedding of Lady
Emeline and her Captain, which took place some two weeks
after the date of the impromptu evening-party there. Much to
her family's susprise, Lady Emeline had decided upon a very
private ceremony, which was perhaps as well, since Lord Arun
refused to give her away and Colin, endeavouring to look much
older than his sixteen years in an extremely dandified neckcloth
and shirtpoints of such inordinate height that he was entirely
precluded from turning his head, had to be pressed into service
as his surrogate.

Miss Trimingham, the governess, writing to Regina to inform
her of the time when she and Nannie Payn would be arriving in
London with their charges (none of the Stacpooles ever wrote
letters except in the direst of emergencies, and usually not even
then), stated circumspectly that Lady Maria and the Honourable
Giles had behaved very well at the wedding, and that Lady
Emeline had looked lovely in amber crape and a straw-coloured
velvet hat trimmed with feathers. Prudently, she forbore to mention that the Honourable Giles, abandoned briefly to his own de-
vices outside the church, had accepted a challenge to battle from
a village urchin from which he had emerged with a gloriously
black eye and a torn jacket, and that Lady Maria had equally
disgraced herself by pummelling a young relation of the urchin's

who had attempted to interfere in the combat. Miss Trimingham was well aware that, if Regina were to flinch from the task of entertaining the young Stacpooles in Cavendish Square, she herself would be left without allies except for Nannie, since even the inadequate young man who served as Colin's tutor had been dismissed, in a final explosion of temper, by Lord Arun before his lordship had departed for Mexico, and she was taking no chances of queering the game. Mrs. Audwyn, Nannie had confided to her, was a young lady with a mind of her own and a way with her young cousins, and that, in Miss Trimingham's opinion, was enough to absolve one of any deception required to enlist her on one's side.

Meanwhile, Regina, with the assistance of her own old governess, Miss Abthorpe, a very capable and highly devoted gentlewoman of sixty whom Regina had taken to live with her when she had been left so young a widow that convention demanded she not reside alone, had been engaged in opening the house in Cavendish Square and making her preparations for the Season that was about to begin. The task was an arduous one, and she was grateful for the assistance provided her by Lord Arun's Mr. Pipping, a dry little gentleman who appeared quite capable, when occasion required, of dealing summarily with recalcitrant Registry Offices, provisioners, and tradesmen. The result was that a competent staff was soon assembled, draperies and upholstery were refurbished or replaced, and the house in Cavendish Square in a remarkably short space of time assumed the appearance of the residence of a family about to introduce a young lady into Society.

The house itself, an extravagance of Lord Arun's, since he disliked it and seldom spent any of his time there, was very grand, with a Roman entrance hall, a great many ancestral portraits in gilded frames, massive chandeliers, and windows draped in colours inclining strongly towards crimson and gold. Regina, whose remembrances of it were not of the happiest, for it was indelibly associated in her mind with the year of her come-out, when it had been lent to her mother by her uncle for the Season, was rather glad on the whole that it would soon be full of young Stacpooles. Even now she could scarcely enter the drawing room without seeing Etienne Audwyn—an elegant figure in impeccable town-dress, an expression of slight boredom upon his dark Gallic face—seated there, making polite conversation with her mama, while she herself, a schoolgirl just turned seventeen, had sat worshipful and tongue-tied in a corner.

It was in that very drawing room, in fact, that she had received Etienne's offer of marriage. Of course, instructed by her mama and impelled by her own dazzled heart, she had accepted him—and of course, she thought, the marriage had been a disaster. A vain, fickle, jaded man of the world and a schoolgirl whom he had married because the time had come for him to settle himself in life. . . . But the same thing would not happen to Bella, she promised herself with determination once more.

The Stacpoole contingent arrived in London in the first week of May. The top floor, where a nursery and schoolroom had been improvised, was promptly taken over by Maria and Giles, who by nightfall were on familiar terms with all the servants, had caused an underfootman to smuggle one of the stable cat's kittens up to them quite unlawfully in a brass can presumed to contain hot water, and had described to Regina so often and so graphically how Giles had been sick on the boat that she was obliged at last to forbid them to speak of it again. But as this prohibition was coupled with an agreement to allow Miss Trimingham to take them the very next day to see Madame Tussaud's Waxworks and the lions and tigers at Exeter 'Change, to say nothing of a promise to procure tickets for the Grand Romantic Spectacle of the Cataract of the Ganges, supported by a Double Tight-Rope performance and an equestrian exhibition, at Astley's Royal Amphitheatre, the two youngest Stacpooles retired to bed very well satisfied with their lot in life.

Peace thereupon reigned in the nursery until midnight, when the kitten made its presence known and was banished once more to the stables by the intermediation of a wrathful Nannie and a very sleepy footman—"me having strong feelings about humans and brute beasts living under the same roof, Miss Regina, as you well know," Nannie, a stupendous vision in yards of cotton flannel and an unexpectedly coquettish night-cap tied with pink ribbons under her ample chin, had stated firmly when Regina, roused by the commotion, had come upstairs to see what was going on.

On the following morning Miss Trimingham set off after breakfast with her two young charges and a somewhat reluctant Colin (who was loth to admit that a person of his advanced age could be as interested in seeing wild animals and waxworks as his young brother and sister but was betrayed by his baser self into bearing them company), and Regina ordered out the carriage to take her and Bella to the establishment of Madame Lafond, a fashionable Bruton Street modiste. Here the two young ladies spent an agreeable pair of hours in an elegant showroom furnished with glittering chandeliers, Aubusson carpets, and thin, gilded chairs, choosing what seemed to a dazzled Bella an extravagant number of gowns for her forthcoming debut into Society.

She was not so dazzled, however, as not to remind Regina of Lord Arun's express injunction to provide herself at his expense with a suitable wardrobe for the Season, and Madame Lafond, delighted at the prospect of dressing a young lady whose elegant tournure would set off her most recherché creations and whose status did not confine her to the demure muslins and cambrics suitable for a girl in her first Season, proceeded to exhibit such a collection of ravishing Italian silks, shimmering satins, feather-light gauzes, and gossamer laces that Regina, almost against her will, was persuaded into allowing herself to be rigged out (Bella's words) quite as lavishly as her young cousin.

"You look simply *famous!*" said Bella, surveying with unfeigned admiration her cousin's reflexion in the tall cheval glass before which she stood, wearing a robe of jonquil silk which clung to her slender figure in the daring fashion of the day and revealed her white neck and shoulders in a most delectable manner. "I'll lay you anything you like that you'll beat everyone else all to sticks when you wear that gown, and have men falling over one another to dance with you!" She went on, speaking even more frankly as Madame Lafond went off to instruct one of her underlings to fetch a fluted pelerine she particularly fancied with the jonquil gown, "Colin and I were talking about that on the way over on the boat: we both think we ought to find a husband for you this Season. I mean to say, you may never have a better opportunity, especially since *I* already have Alistair, so that you will be able to spend all your time looking for someone for yourself."

Regina said, smiling at her young cousin in the glass, "Well, I'm sure that is very kind of you and Colin, but would you mind a great deal if we forget all about my matrimonial prospects *and* Lord Wrexam for the Season and concentrate instead on seeing that you enjoy your come-out?"

"But we can't do *that,*" Bella, who could see the door from where she sat, said reasonably. "Forget about Alistair, I mean. Because here he comes now."

Regina turned swiftly. Bella had spoken the truth: Madame Lafond was indeed ushering Lord Wrexam into the room at that very moment. A superlatively fitting coat of Bath superfine, biscuit pantaloons, and gleaming, gold-tasselled Hessians set off his tall figure to excellent advantage, and he looked quite as much at home in this elegant white-and-gold showroom as if he were thoroughly accustomed to visiting the establishments of fashionable modistes.

"Which I expect he is—along with the current barque of frailty he has under his protection!" Regina thought indignantly, observing the air of slightly coquettish and extremely deferential familiarity with which Madame was addressing him. "Good God! I hope she has not taken the idea into her head that Bella is one of his ladybirds—or that I am!"

But she need have had no fear of Wrexam's casting the slightest slur upon either her own or her cousin's respectability. His lordship, Madame said volubly, had explained that he had just come from Cavendish Square, where he had been informed that the ladies had gone out to visit her establishment.

"And Milord says," she went on, looking, Regina thought, very French and incredibly coy, "that, as there is soon to be a family connexion *de la plus intime* between himself and the young ladies, he felt it might be considered quite *comme il faut* for him to stop and pay his respects, and enquire if there were perhaps any small commission he might execute—"

"If you will kindly," Regina said to Madame in what she

hoped was a quelling voice, "see to having the pelerine fetched, Madame—? I am afraid we have very little more time." And as Madame, all apologies, hurried out, she went on warmly to Wrexam, "How *dared* you say such a thing to her?"

Wrexam raised a quizzical black brow at her, and lifted his glass the better to scrutinise the jonquil silk gown.

"Admirable!" he said, when he had completed his leisurely inspection. "I hope you intend to purchase it."

"That, Lord Wrexam, is certainly none of your affair! And you *haven't* answered my question."

"Your question? Ah, yes! How dared I tell Lafond that I had been to call upon you in Cavendish Square? But I had, you know."

"You know very well that is *not* what I meant! How did you have the—the unmitigated audacity to tell her that there would soon be a family connexion between you and ourselves—?"

"My dear girl," said Wrexam, in his maddeningly imperturbable manner, "pray consider the advantages of presenting the matter to the world as a *fait accompli*. It brings the weight of public opinion to bear upon your uncle—not, I imagine," he added thoughtfully, "that that has ever carried much weight with him—"

"No, it has not!" Regina said roundly. "And, for my own part, I warn you, Lord Wrexam, that I shall certainly contradict such a story if you put it about."

"No—will you?" said Wrexam, with interest. "Does that mean you will tell Lafond that I am actually an untruthful and untrustworthy fellow, who was merely cutting a sham with her? Here she comes now, so you have your opportunity—"

Madame bustled in, followed by an assistant bearing the pelerine. The assistant draped it deftly over Regina's shoulders, and Regina, to her intense discomposure, found herself being regarded approvingly and expectantly by four pairs of eyes, one pair, at least, full of wicked amusement.

"Well?" said Wrexam encouragingly.

"Well?" echoed Madame eagerly, pursuing her own train of thought. "*C'est jolie, n'est-ce pas?* And becomes Madame *à ravir!*"

She appealed to Wrexam, who remarked promptly that in his opinion she was quite right.

"I shall look forward to seeing you wearing it—perhaps at the Subscription Ball at Almack's on Wednesday?" he said to Regina. "You *have* obtained vouchers for Lady Arabella, have you not?"

Regina wished with all her heart that she might be able to say that she had, for she was well aware of the prime importance of obtaining entree to the "Marriage Mart," as this most exclusive of London clubs was sometimes irreverently called, for any young lady aspiring to a successful come-out. But in her persevering efforts during the past few weeks to renew her acquaintance with those ladies of *ton* who could be most useful to her in promoting Bella's career in Society, she had not yet succeeded in meeting any of the few august Patronesses of Almack's who had already arrived in town for the Season. As she was not personally upon terms of intimacy with any of them, she had felt that it would be looked upon as presumptuous were she to write to Lady Sefton, for example, and request her, on the basis of a few brief meetings several years ago, to provide her with the coveted vouchers for her protégée. Wrexam apparently observed her hesitation, for he said no more at the moment upon the subject.

When they were outside upon the flagway, however, with a pair of shop assistants hastening to carry their purchases to the waiting barouche, he returned to the matter.

"I take it," he remarked, "by your silence on the subject, that you have not yet obtained vouchers to Almack's for Lady Arabella, Mrs. Audwyn. Perhaps I might be of service to you there. I am rather well acquainted with Sally Jersey, and I am tolerably certain that if I were to request her—"

"—to furnish vouchers for *your betrothed?*" Regina interrupted him. "And have it spread all over the town within four-and-twenty hours that Bella *is* actually engaged to you? No, I thank you, Lord Wrexam! We shall manage very well without that particular sort of help!"

She moved away from him and mounted into the barouche, signalling to Bella to follow her. Bella looked mutinous.

"Reggie, don't be *twitty!*" she said. "Alistair is only trying to be obliging!"

"Alas, my child," Wrexam said wryly, "your cousin reads me far better than you do!" He looked up at Regina with a faint smile upon his lips, raising his hand in the gesture of a fencer acknowledging a hit. "Very well," he said. "I shall abandon that game, Mrs. Audwyn. But if I promise—word of honour!—to present Lady Arabella's claims to admission to Almack's merely upon the basis of my friendship with Lord Arun (who fortunately will not be here to dispute my words), may I have your consent to speak to Lady Jersey on the subject?"

Regina looked at him irresolutely. It would certainly be to Bella's advantage, she knew, if Wrexam, whose acquaintance in the *ton* was far more extensive than Regina's own, were to take a hand in smoothing her young protégée's social path; on the other hand, she did not in the least wish to be beholden to him. He saw her hesitation, and the slight air of distress, which she could not entirely hide, occasioned by her genuine uncertainty as to what course she ought to pursue, and an odd look came into his own cynical dark eyes.

"Good Lord!" he said, oblivious for the moment, it seemed, to the presence of the coachman upon the box of the open carriage. "I believe you are really in earnest about all this! It isn't merely a matter of my having set your back up, or of your choosing to humour Arun in this ridiculous maggot he has taken into his head—"

"It is *not* ridiculous, Lord Wrexam," Regina said in a low voice. "He is quite right. Bella is too young, too inexperienced— Believe me, I know—" She cast a glance at the coachman and broke off. "I am sorry," she said, in an even lower voice. "I can't discuss it here."

"May I return with you to Cavendish Square and discuss it there?" Wrexam demanded.

She shook her head silently and ordered the coachman to drive on. But for some reason she felt oddly shaken by this interchange, and Bella's indignant lamentations over her refusal to allow Wrexam to accompany them back to Cavendish Square did little to put her in a quieter frame of mind. She could only wish distractedly that some paragon of masculine eligibility and beauty would soon come into her young cousin's life who would instantly cause her to turn from Wrexam and fix her affections upon him, for that it would be quite impossible for her to prevent Bella from meeting the ubiquitous Earl here in London had now become abundantly clear to her.

When they arrived in Cavendish Square they found that Miss Trimingham and the younger Stacpooles had already returned from their morning excursion. Miss Abthorpe, whom Regina came upon in the hall, reported that Miss Trimingham had been obliged by Giles and Maria, under threat of public misbehaviour, to purchase a rat-trap from a vendor selling those useful articles in the street, and that they were now in the kitchen engaged in begging cheese with which to bait it from the cook.

"I should have put a stop to that soon enough if I had seen it would upset him," said Miss Abthorpe, who knew the difficulties of procuring a genuine French chef as well as anyone in London, "but it was no such thing, my dear. They have got round him just as they have got round the rest of the servants, and he was showing them how to make timbales when I came in. All your young relations," she added somewhat severely, "seem to have a great deal of charm."

"Yes, and they are *quite* unscrupulous about using it," Regina agreed. "Never mind; if Pierre becomes fond of them, perhaps he won't give notice, after all. I have a lowering feeling that he considers the amount of entertaining I have done up to the present time quite beneath him."

"Which reminds me," said Miss Abthorpe, brightening a little, "that you had a pair of callers while you were out. The Comte de Chelles and the Chevalier de Lescot. Relations of your late husband, I believe? They seemed very much disappointed not to find you in and said they would call again tomorrow."

Regina looked at her in some surprise. "The Comte de Chelles?" she repeated slowly, as she attempted to sort out the identities of the callers in her mind. "Why, yes—he is my husband's maternal uncle. But I have never met him, and I hadn't the least notion he was in England. I always understood he chose to return to France under the amnesty after the Revolution, and became an official of quite some importance under Bonaparte."

"Oh, my dear—no!" Miss Abthorpe said, looking shocked, for her standards, like those of all good governesses, were far more severe than those of the highest stickler among the class that employed her when it came to the conduct to be expected from them. "I cannot think," she continued, "that any connexion of yours, French though he may be, would so far forget what was due to his birth as to consort with that Corsican monster!"

"But I am very much afraid that he did, you know," Regina said, smiling a little at Miss Abthorpe's scandalised face. "After all, I daresay it cannot have been very comfortable for him, living in exile with all his estates confiscated. Only of course it has done him no good in the end, for with Bonaparte overthrown and the Bourbons back on the throne of France, I expect he must be ruined all over again. I wonder that he has decided to come to England, for even with the war over he can scarcely expect to be welcomed here—"

Colin's voice said behind her in a very grown-up way that he rather fancied she was about to be saddled with a pair of dirty dishes.

"No, really, Colin!" she protested, turning to see him come strolling down the last of the stairs, the man-of-the-world effect he was evidently striving for somewhat spoiled by the fact that he was munching an apple with a schoolboy's relish. "It can't be so bad as that!"

"Dirty dishes," Colin repeated firmly. "I caught a glimpse of them as we came in. Rather a seedy-looking fellow, the older one, with a pair of black eyes that bore into you like gimlets. The younger one," he admitted tolerantly, "has quite a nice taste in waistcoats. A bit austere, perhaps—but that's to be preferred, of course, over the gaudy."

Miss Abthorpe, who had a very direct way of dealing with the young, told him in a composed manner that he knew nothing of the matter, and then looked at him in such a pointed way as she remarked that luncheon would soon be served that all his pretensions deserted him and, self-conscious concerning the state of cleanliness of ears, neck, and hands as he had not been since nursery days, he went hastily off to remedy any defects of this nature.

"A very nice boy," Miss Abthorpe remarked sedately to Regina. "Needs taking down a bit, but then they all do. And quite right, of course, about the Comte's appearance, though it is not my place to say it, *nor* his, if it comes to that."

"Oh, dear!" said Regina. "Perhaps he *does* intend to settle here in England and wishes me to help him to establish himself. And, really, you know, Abby, though I am sorry for him, of course, I don't *need* any more complications just now!"

"Well, I daresay one could keep saying you are not at home when he calls, but he would be bound to come up with you sooner or later if he is really determined to see you, so I expect you had as well admit him when he calls tomorrow," Miss Abthorpe said bracingly. "And the Chevalier," she added with an entirely unexpected air of definite appreciation, "is really an extraordinarily handsome young man. Excellent manners, too. A nephew of the Comte's, I understand?"

Regina said she had not the least notion; Etienne had spoken so infrequently to her of his French relations that she had no idea of the family ramifications. As Maria and Giles appeared just then from the kitchen, triumphantly bearing a piece of cheese large enough to have tempted an army of rats, had any of that abhorrent species been present in the house to suffer temptation, she had no opportunity to go into the matter further at the moment, however; and in the excitement of opening the bandboxes she and Bella had brought with them from Madame Lafond's, hearing from the younger Stacpooles the story of their morning's excursion, and discussing the list of guests who had been invited to the ball to be given shortly in Bella's honour, the afternoon, too, passed without any further allusion to the French visitors.

CHAPTER
5

On the following day Regina was a good deal surprised to receive a morning call from Lady Jersey. Of course she at once saw Wrexam's hand in the matter—no doubt he had paid not the least heed to her openly expressed dislike of his approaching the Queen of the London *ton* upon Bella's behalf—and it was therefore with a considerably heightened colour and a manner lacking something of her usual poise that she greeted the Countess upon the latter's entrance into the drawing room.

Her composure was not improved when, the usual civilities having been exchanged, Lady Jersey, who had been subjecting her to a penetrating scrutiny, suddenly said frankly, "You must forgive me for staring so shamelessly, my dear, but I will confess to being consumed by curiosity as to the attractions of the young lady who could induce Wrexam to abandon the habits of a lifetime and not only solicit my interest in promoting the social career of her protégée, but even engage to appear at Almack's himself if I obliged him by doing so. He finds our balls abominably flat, you know—masses of young girls just out of the schoolroom, and nothing but tea and lemonade to drink, not to speak of the gaming being only for chicken-stakes! But I must admit that, even now that I have seen you, I am still most dreadfully curious. Not that you are not *quite* lovely, and charming, and all the other adjectives so often bestowed on young ladies who don't deserve them half so much as you do—but you are not at all in his style, you know!"

Regina, who had been vainly endeavouring to interrupt the flow of her ladyship's talk ever since the first astonishing hint had been thrown out that it was she, and not Bella, who was presumed to be the object of Lord Wrexam's interest, here suddenly found herself with the floor and simultaneously discovered that she had nothing to say. At least she could think of nothing that would be a proper and dignified rebuke to Wrexam for having turned the tables upon her in this dastardly way.

Still she *must*, she thought, say *something*, or, knowing Lady Jersey's reputation, she might be assured that the rumour that Wrexam was *épris* with her would be one of the *on-dits* of the town before another four-and-twenty hours had passed.

And then, almost before that thought had had time to flash into her mind, another idea followed it with equal swiftness. It would serve Lord Wrexam exactly right, ran this idea, if she were to allow Lady Jersey to think precisely what she was now thinking, and to publish it to the world if she wished. If his lordship chose to throw out quite improper hints as to a forthcoming connexion between himself and the members of the Cavendish Square household, as he had done at Madame Lafond's establishment, he would find that two could play at that game.

All this passed through her mind in the space of seconds, and before Lady Jersey could begin to wonder at her silence she had folded her hands in her lap, bent her head modestly, and murmured that she had indeed had the pleasure of renewing her acquaintance with Lord Wrexam upon the occasion of a visit to Ireland a few weeks before.

"But I am quite sure that you are mistaken, ma'am," she said, in the tone of a young lady who is sure of nothing of the sort, "in believing that *I* can have had any influence upon his conduct. Perhaps," she went on, wishing very much that his lordship were there to hear her, "he has come to an age when he himself realises that it may be time for him to alter his way of life—"

"Wrexam?" said Lady Jersey incredulously. "My dear, if you believe that, you are green indeed! He is an incorrigible rake and gamester and always will be, unless—as sometimes happens, even with men of *his* stamp—he has the good fortune to meet the one woman in the world who can wind him round her little finger. And now that I come to think of it," her ladyship said thoughtfully, "unlikely as it seems, you may indeed be that woman! I have seen it happen before, I assure you. It is a man like Wrexam, who has had his fill of dashing Birds of Paradise, who is most often caught in the end by a cool, elegant creature like yourself! Still it is the greatest jest in the world to think of it, for he has always been dreadfully impatient of clever women, and you *are* clever, my dear; I can see it in your face."

Was she clever? By this time Regina was beginning to doubt it very much. She had spoken, upon impulse, the words that had confirmed Lady Jersey in her notion of Wrexam's interest in her, but already she was regretting that impulse. She began to imagine his lordship's reaction when he learned that he was being confidently rumoured to be a fervent suitor for her hand, and, furthermore, that she herself had not only made no attempt to deny that rumour, but had behaved in such a way as to confirm it. And the more she imagined, the more uneasy she became.

"Well, it is his own fault!" she thought, with some spirit. "If he had not begun this odious game, I should never have had the chance to go on with it. And, at any rate, it may do *some* good, in that it will make any connexion between him and Bella appear far less probable."

What Bella herself would think when she learned of the rumour she did not dare to consider, and, in any event, the arrival of the Comte de Chelles and the Chevalier de Lescot just on the heels of the departure of Lady Jersey, who left promising in the most good-natured way to send the coveted vouchers, allowed her no opportunity to do so.

The moment these two gentlemen entered the room she was able to see that the description she had been given of them by Colin and Miss Abthorpe had been an extremely apt one. The younger of her callers was a dark, excessively handsome young man of perhaps five- or six-and-twenty, with easy manners and an air of modestly self-assured competence that Regina liked at once. His companion, on the other hand, who was about sixty, and had iron-grey hair, startlingly black brows, and the oddly penetrating eyes of which Colin had spoken, was far less prepossessing; and she had the rather uncomfortable feeling, as he bowed over her hand, that he was subjecting her to a scrutiny of quite unusual intensity.

When he spoke, however, his voice was smooth and deferential.

"*Chère Madame*—such a pleasure to meet at last poor Etienne's wife! And such grief to me when I learned at last—long after the event—of his death! A hunting accident, I believe? *Quel malheur!* A young man still, in the flower of his manhood—"

Regina, inured by her residence on the Continent to the foreign lack of reticence on subjects she herself would much prefer not to hear discussed, gave brief replies to the Comte's effusive lamentations, which she was obliged to believe must be based more upon a general family feeling than upon any more personal grief, since it appeared that he had had only a slight acquaintance with his deceased nephew. He had not, in fact, it seemed, so much as set eyes upon him since the two had met in '02 in Vienna, where the Comte had been living in exile during the Revolution—a meeting that had apparently occurred just before the Comte had resolved to take advantage of the amnesty being offered to the members of the nobility by Bonaparte and return to France.

For some reason, Regina thought, the Comte wished to lay particular stress upon this last meeting with his nephew, and his ordinarily intense and gimletlike (to use Colin's simile) black eyes looked so much more intense and gimletlike as he referred to it that she began to wonder if there was something peculiar about him, which would not, possibly, be a matter for surprise in view of the vicissitudes he had suffered during the past few decades of his life. She began to wish fervently that Miss Abthorpe or Bella would come in. In the slight nervousness she felt about the Comte's odd behaviour, she turned her attention rather pointedly to the Chevalier, who had remained civilly silent during her interchange with her elder visitor, and enquired if he had been long in England.

"On the contrary—only for a few days," replied the Chevalier.

"My uncle and I arrived in Bristol on Thursday from New Orleans."

"From New Orleans?" Regina looked at him with interest. "Then you have been living in America—?"

"Yes. My father emigrated, you see, in the first years of the Revolution, when I was only a child. And so, if you please, I am plain Mr. Lescot, an American citizen, and no longer the Chevalier de Lescot—"

Regina said she had always wished to see New Orleans, which seemed to her the most romantic place in the world if one didn't die of yellow fever or malaria or whatever it was one got there, and asked Lescot if he intended to go on living there, now that Bonaparte had been deposed for good.

"Oh, yes!" he said. "I am a thoroughgoing American now. I have a plantation near New Orleans that may some day do very well for me, and I enjoy the life—"

"Ah," interrupted the Comte suddenly, "he is too modest, *chère Madame!* He does very well for himself in America now— *ca se voit!* I myself was astonished, when I arrived in New Orleans a year ago from France, to find my young kinsman so fortunately situated, quite as if my poor brother and his wife had not lost everything in the Revolution. Alas! They were both dead when I—an exile now for the second time in my life—arrived in New Orleans with no more than the clothes upon my back. But my good Gervais"—he bent a look of saturnine approval upon young Mr. Lescot—"behaved to me *en vrai fils*—how do you say it?—as if he were my son. My health, you understand, has been far from good, but how could I but recover in a most comfortable house, surrounded by every attention and fortified by the care and solicitude of this excellent young man?"

Lescot, meeting Regina's eyes at this point, smiled faintly and gave a slight, despairing shrug of his shoulders, but so good-humouredly that her opinion of him rose again and she smiled at him in return.

"I am sure," she said to the Comte politely, "you do not exaggerate in the least," and then met Lescot's eyes once more and smiled as she saw slight colour mount in his cheeks. A refreshingly normal, pleasant young man, she thought, in spite of his ro-

mantic good looks, and asked him if he had any other acquaintances in London.

His answer was reassuring, in view of her previous specula-
tions as to whether her French visitors might require her assistance in making their way in England. Lescot, it appeared, had
come to London armed with letters of introduction to several
persons of the highest rank and consequence in the *ton;* he had
called the previous day upon two of them, Lord Alvanley and
the Countess Lieven, wife of the Russian Ambassador and one of
the Patronesses of Almack's, and as a result had already been
taken by the former to White's, where he had met a great many
of Alvanley's friends, and been bidden by the Countess to attend
the Subscription Ball at Almack's on the following night, where
he might, she had told him, meet all the reigning Beauties of
London Society.

"Which of course," Regina said, with her sudden look of mischief, "you are eager to do," and at that moment Bella came into
the room.

The gentlemen were introduced and Bella sat down—not very
willingly, however, it seemed, for she was wearing her riding-
dress and took the opportunity very soon to remind Regina audibly that she had promised they might go for a ride in the Park
that morning.

"Bella has no manners," Regina said soothingly to young Lescot, who had stiffened slightly at this bald hint and had begun at
once to say that they must go. "She was reared, you see, upon
the principle that they are a useless encumbrance, happily dis-
pensed with by the noble savages who inhabit the wilder parts
of your country, Mr. Lescot."

Lescot said that, on the contrary, all the savages he had ever
seen had very formal manners, in their own way quite as cere-
monious as any to be found in *ton* circles, upon which Bella
looked a little superior and asked him if he had read Rousseau.

"Yes!" said Lescot uncompromisingly; but meanwhile, as the
two young people confronted each other in some animosity, the
Comte had risen from his chair and now approached Regina.

"*Chère Madame*—a word in your ear, *s'il vous plaît*," he said, his black eyes fixing themselves upon her face with such earnestness that she was again conscious of that slight feeling of uneasiness. "You will perhaps have guessed *à propos de quoi—hein?*" he suggested, sitting down beside her upon the sofa and speaking in her ear. "The matter of the necklace—?"

He looked at her significantly, appearing to anticipate an immediate response. Regina looked at him enquiringly.

"The necklace?" she repeated.

"*Mais oui!*" said the Comte impatiently. "The Chelles diamonds. The necklace that was left by me in your husband's safekeeping!"

Regina stared at him in bewilderment. She had not the faintest idea what he was talking of, but she saw, by the look of suspicion that was now overspreading his face, that he considered her air of ignorance merely feigned.

"Come, come, my dear!" he said, even more brusquely than before. "There is no need for you to speak otherwise than frankly to me! You must know the history of those diamonds quite as well as I do! They were entrusted by me to Etienne on the occasion of our last meeting in Vienna; I was understandably reluctant, *vous savez*, after I had once succeeded in leaving France with them in '93, to hazard them again in the country when I returned, before I had been able to ascertain what conditions were there. And by the time I was able to make arrangements to have the necklace returned to me, war had broken out again between France and England, so that it was impossible for me to have any further communication with Etienne on the matter. I have always remained confident, however, of his faithfulness to his trust, and now that the trust has descended to you—"

"But it *hasn't* descended to me!" Regina protested, still quite at sea. "Believe me, Monsieur, I have never heard of the necklace before this moment! And I have no notion what Etienne can have done with it, for he never spoke of it to me—"

"He left a will—*hein?*" the Comte demanded.

Regina shook her head. "No," she said. "He died very suddenly, you see, and his affairs were left in the greatest disorder.

There were a good many debts, and—in short, Monsieur, I am quite certain that if the necklace had been discovered among his effects his creditors would have demanded—"

"Yes, yes!" the Comte cut her off. "But there are ways of concealing something as small as a necklace, *chère Madame!* And this necklace, you understand, was not his to dispose of. It is a family heirloom of extraordinary value, and I can well believe that Etienne, if he were indeed as hard-pressed financially as you imply, might have taken extraordinary care to keep it from falling into the hands of unauthorised persons. There is the house in Upper Wimpole Street, for example. You have not searched for it there?"

"The house in Upper Wimpole Street?" *He must be quite mad!* Regina was thinking, with conviction. "What house, my dear Comte? And how can I have searched for a necklace I had never heard of in a house I have never seen?" The Comte continued to stare at her with unforgiving suspicion. "Do you mean you believe Etienne owned a house in Upper Wimpole Street?" Regina asked, casting an appealing glance across the room at Mr. Lescot, who might be able to help her, she thought, in soothing the Comte's madness. But Lescot was immersed in what seemed a rather warm dispute with Bella and remained quite impervious to the look.

"Owned it?" the Comte was saying, meanwhile. "Not at all! But it has been leased by him, certainly, under the name of Mr. Baker, since the year 1810. Of this you are not aware?"

"Of this I am not at all aware!" Regina said, feeling more dazed than ever. "*Has* been leased, you say. But you can't mean it is still—? My dear Comte, Etienne has been dead for over two years!"

"Yes, yes—but the lease remains. The rent is paid punctually by his solicitors, Messieurs Copplestone, Copplestone, and Thripp," the Comte said, managing the English names with some difficulty. "I have had enquiries made; there is not the least doubt. You know Messieurs Copplestone, Copplestone, and Thripp?" he demanded.

Regina, with a rising sense of panic, said automatically that she believed the Mr. Copplestone she had met over the matter of Etienne's estate was dead, and that his son was now the principal in the firm.

"Then I suggest," said the Comte decisively, "that you enquire of him concerning this house. You will, of course," he went on, fixing her sternly with his black eyes, "be prepared to return the necklace to its rightful owner if it is discovered there? I may depend upon you in that?"

"But of course," Regina said helplessly, "you must certainly have it if it is found and indeed belongs to you. But I—"

"*Mais non!*" said the Comte firmly. "You are about to say that you do not believe in the existence of either the house *or* the necklace. Be assured, however, *chère Madame*, that both *do* exist." He rose. "Now I shall impose no longer upon your kindness," he said. "I shall leave you, and you will go at once to Messieurs Copplestone, Copplestone, and Thripp. *Je vous implore!* Seek out this house; search there for the necklace; return to an old and honoured house this last memento of its former greatness! Madame, I now bid you good-day. Come, Gervais."

He bowed, swept Lescot off with him with an imperative lift of his startlingly black brows, and was gone. Regina, feeling as if she had just emerged from a madhouse, looked blankly across the room at Bella.

"What an *extraordinary* man!" she said.

"Well, as I didn't exchange above two words with him, I cannot judge," Bella said, her cheeks very pink and an ireful expression upon her pretty face. "But if he is anything like his nephew, 'extraordinary' is far too good a word for him! *He* is certainly the most abominably conceited, opinionated—"

"Mr. Lescot? But I thought him a particularly agreeable young man," Regina said distractedly. "His uncle, though, is certainly quite mad, or I have been landed in the midst of the strangest bumblebath I have ever heard of!"

And she proceeded to disclose to her young cousin the substance of her conversation with the Comte, which had the effect of diverting Bella's mind immediately from her incipient feud with Mr. Lescot. In the middle of the story Colin strolled in from a morning very profitably spent in viewing a peep show in Coventry Street and visiting Bullock's Museum, where Napoleon's carriage was on display, and the tale had to be repeated from the beginning for his benefit.

As befitted his position as a budding man of the world and the instant distrust he had conceived of the Comte, he chose to take a cynical view of the matter.

"Ten to one it's all a hum," he said confidently. "What should Etienne have wanted with a house in Upper Wimpole Street that you never heard of? It doesn't make the slightest degree of sense!"

"Perhaps he had another wife there," Bella suggested hopefully. "Men *do* sometimes, you know."

Colin looked at her witheringly. "My poor child, *not* Etienne!" he said. "By all I ever heard, it was as much as his family could do to get him to the altar *once.*"

"What a horrid thing to say!" Bella said indignantly. "Don't mind him, Reggie. He really *is* a beast!"

"The thing is," Colin went on, ignoring this sisterly interruption, "what are we to do now? *I* think we should go to see Messrs. Thingummy, Thingummy, and Thripp at once. At least they'll be able to tell us if it's all a bag of moonshine about this house affair—"

"Well, *I* certainly must see them; there is no doubt of that," Regina said. "Only if it turns out that there really *is* a house in Upper Wimpole Street, that still doesn't in the least prove that there is a necklace there. And if it shouldn't be there, and the Comte takes it into his head I am concealing it—"

"He may come creeping into the house at midnight and try to murder you in your bed to get it from you," Colin said enthusiastically, suddenly becoming his proper age again. "I say, that *would* be an adventure! Perhaps I'd best get hold of a pistol—"

"You will do nothing of the sort," Regina said firmly. "Good heavens, you absurd boy, the Comte is a nobleman of France; eccentric he may well be, but he is assuredly not so eccentric as *that.*"

She got up briskly and said she must change into her riding-dress at once if they were to ride that morning; but as she went upstairs she could not help wishing that the Comte de Chelles and his nephew had remained in New Orleans. Nothing but trouble, it seemed, was to come of their sudden appearance in London.

CHAPTER

6

On the following morning Regina paid an early visit to the offices of Messrs. Copplestone, Copplestone, and Thripp in the Strand. She had had, as she had informed the Comte, some dealings with the elder Mr. Copplestone—a dry, precise old gentleman, much in the style of Lord Arun's Mr. Pipping—at the time of Etienne's death, but she had never visited his place of business nor met the other members of the firm.

An elderly clerk, whose very back seemed to express his disapproval of the appearance of a female in this masculine sanctum, left his high stool to go upstairs and announce her arrival to the younger Mr. Copplestone, and in a few moments Mr. Thomas Copplestone himself came down to her. He was a tall, vague man with pale, astonished-looking blue eyes and a confiding manner.

"My dear Mrs. Audwyn," he greeted her anxiously, "there is nothing *wrong*, is there? I do so hope there is nothing wrong?"

He took her hand rather distrustfully in his and gave it back to her at once. Regina said not exactly wrong, but there was some information she wished very much he might be able to give her.

"Information?" said Mr. Copplestone doubtfully. "Well, I daresay I *might*—You see, things *have* got into something of a muddle since my father left us—" He saw that the elderly clerk was regarding him with a dour and steely eye and said hastily to

Regina, "But you had best come up to my office, hadn't you? I mean, if you really *do* have something you wish to ask me—"

Regina, with the feeling that both she and Mr. Copplestone were in disgrace, thankfully escaped with him up a breakneck pair of stairs and soon found herself ensconced in an ancient carved armchair in a very disorderly room, which smelled strongly of leather and snuff.

"*Not* a room for a lady," Mr. Copplestone said unhappily, looking around it as if he had never seen it before and was as astonished as she was to find it so untidy. "You wouldn't believe, I expect, that in my father's day it was as neat as a pin. I *do* try, but I find that if I let anyone put things away where they think they ought to be, then they aren't where *I* think they ought to be any more—"

Regina, seeing that he was apparently well launched upon a lengthy explanation *cum* apology, said soothingly that she was sure it was all a great deal of trouble to him, but could he perhaps provide her with the information she had come for, and then she would not be obliged to take up his time any longer.

"It is about a house in Upper Wimpole Street," she said. "A house upon which my husband presumably had a lease—"

"Up-per Wim-pole Street," said Mr. Copplestone, as tentatively as if he had never heard that particular combination of syllables before. "Up-per Wim-pole Street." His face brightened suddenly. "I once had an aunt who lived there," he confided. "Shocking Tartar she was. Frightened everyone into fits. But she's been dead for years. Years and years and—" His voice trailed off in meditative remembrance.

"The house I am speaking of," Regina said firmly, "was leased by my husband in 1810, under the name of Baker, I understand. Copplestone, Copplestone, and Thripp handled the payment of the rent. Indeed, I have been told they still continue to do so."

"Baker," Mr. Copplestone said thoughtfully, and then, rapidly and triumphantly, "Baker, Baker, Baker! I *do* remember! An extraordinary business. Quite an ex-traordinary business!"

He beamed at her as if inviting her to share his satisfaction in his feat of recollection, and Regina, who was beginning to sympathise with the dour exasperation with which the elderly clerk had regarded his employer, asked rather impatiently if he meant to imply that the house was still being leased by the fictitious Mr. Baker.

"Oh, yes. Still being leased. Yes, yes, yes. Quite ex-traordinary," said Mr. Copplestone, nodding his head with the look of satisfaction still upon his face. "I remember it quite as if it were yesterday. Which it wasn't, you know, because it must have been all of half a dozen years ago. I believe you did say 1810?"

"Yes!" said Regina. "Mr. Copplestone, I should like very much to know why my husband rented this house, and why there was this curious arrangement made for him to go on renting it after his death—"

"But he couldn't have *known* he was going to die, could he?" Mr. Copplestone argued, with mild reasonableness. "One doesn't, you know. Of course, I have often thought how much more convenient it would be, say, for a stonemason, for example, in erecting a joint memorial for husband and wife where one of the parties predeceases the other—"

"Mr. Copplestone!" said Regina severely. Mr. Copplestone started and blinked at her reproachfully. "I *don't* wish to be uncivil," Regina went on, "but I *should* like you to tell me exactly what reason my husband gave your father for making this very odd arrangement about the house."

"He didn't give any reason," Mr. Copplestone said, still reproachful. "Honestly, I'd tell you if I knew, Mrs. Audwyn. But I don't. Papa—that is, my father—was quite put out about the whole affair, I remember very well. Mr. Audwyn simply put a sum of money into his hands and said it was to be used to pay the rent on that house for as long as the lease ran, and that no one else was to know about it. And the payments weren't to be discontinued on any account. It will be up very soon—the lease, I mean," he said hopefully. "At least I don't believe there's much left in the fund. But I may be mistaken. I often am," he added rather gloomily.

Regina said it didn't much matter to her when the lease was up, which made him look more cheerful, but then she said that if by any chance he had a key or knew where she might get one she would like very much to see the house, upon which he once more relapsed into gloom.

"I expect there *is* a key," he admitted reluctantly, after a moment. "But I don't know where it is. I'd have to ask Nyce."

"Nyce?"

"Papa's old clerk. The one you met downstairs." He said even more gloomily, "*He*'ll think I ought to know where it is."

"Nonsense!" said Regina encouragingly. "I'm sure no one could expect a man in your position to keep such unimportant details in mind"—*because if I don't humour him,* she thought in despair, *I shall never see the key or the house or anything else!* "Come along; we'll ask him," she said, and led the way down the steep stairs, with Mr. Copplestone, protesting feebly, following behind her.

Nyce, on being appealed to, said austerely that there was indeed a key, but—looking quellingly at Regina—that he shouldn't think it ought to be released except to an authorised person.

"But Mrs. Audwyn *is* authorised," said Mr. Copplestone, apparently plucking up sufficient courage from Regina's presence to defy his clerk. "She's as authorised as anything! She is Mr. Audwyn's wife—or widow, I expect I should say. And *that*," he concluded triumphantly, "is even better, because he *might* not have wished his wife to know about the house, but he *can't* mind if his widow does, because of being dead."

Nyce, who looked as if he had a poor opinion of wives, and widows too, made no reply to this, but rose and went off to fetch the key, while Regina, who was quite certain what idea of the use to which Etienne had put the house in Upper Wimpole Street Mr. Copplestone's last statement had concealed, began to wonder if she was so eager to have the key, after all. She had long since got over her first schoolgirl shock at learning that Etienne had been unfaithful to his marriage vows almost from the moment he had uttered them, but still it would be a far from agreeable experience to be obliged to view the setting in which he had carried out one, or perhaps several, of his transitory affairs.

And then the common sense and knowledge of the world that she had accumulated in the years since that first shock of discovery had overwhelmed her came to her rescue and she almost laughed. It was in the highest degree improbable, she thought, that any of the expensive barques of frailty Etienne had had in keeping would have settled for so unfashionable an address as Upper Wimpole Street. Mr. Copplestone's suspicions to the contrary, there must be another explanation of why her husband had rented a house in that respectable, humdrum neighbourhood, but what it could be she had at present not the faintest notion.

With the key in her hand and her carriage waiting outside, however, there was nothing to stop her from finding out at once anything that the house itself could tell her; but, curiously enough, she found herself still reluctant to embark upon that adventure. It would be better, she told herself with what she felt was a quite cowardly lack of spirit, to take someone with her when she went there—Miss Abthorpe, perhaps, or Colin. And then there was the matter of the fitting Bella was to have that morning at Madame Lafond's: she really ought not allow her to go there without her. Bella had a weakness for ornament, and was quite capable, with her Stacpoole genius for walking over almost anyone on her way to getting what she wanted, of bullying even Madame Lafond into ruining her new pale blue muslin ball dress by loading it with yards of Malines lace or Berlin silk floss.

So she ordered the coachman to drive back to Cavendish Square, instead of sending him on to Upper Wimpole Street, and for the remainder of the day pushed the matter of the house resolutely to the back of her mind. This, in the event, was not difficult to do, for the evening was to bring the ball at which Bella would make her first appearance at Almack's, and that young lady was in such high gig over it that no one else in the house was allowed to talk or think of anything else all day long. Colin, to demonstrate his own lordly contempt for anything so frivolous as a ball, went off presently to further his acquaintance with a young man whom he had met on the previous day, and who not only had the distinction of having been thrown out of Harrow, but had promised to initiate him into such forbidden mysteries of London life as the Cock-pit Royal and the Fives-court. Shortly afterwards, Maria, burning with secret emulation of her elder sister, was found peacocking about in the nursery in Bella's spider-gauze ball gown and Denmark satin slippers, waving the fan of frosted crape on ivory sticks that her sister was to carry that evening; and Giles, attempting to draw off Nannie's ire from Maria's crime, inspirationally emptied the sugar bowl out of the nursery window upon the head of an unfortunate young dandy in a high-crowned beaver who made such a disturbance over it that Hughes was obliged to sally forth and mollify him by taking the injured headgear in hand himself and returning it to him in due time in a state in which its owner no longer felt disgraced to be seen parading beneath it in Cavendish Square.

CHAPTER 7

In such manner the day passed, and Regina was thankful, at an hour shortly before ten, to see Bella step at last into the carriage that was to convey them to the Assembly Rooms in King Street, her gown of white spider-gauze setting off her neat little figure to great advantage, a wreath of pink roses on her shining dark hair, and the fan, rescued from Maria and with the spot of raspberry jam left upon the sticks vengefully scrubbed off by Nannie, dangling from its silk ribbon at her wrist.

Regina herself for some obscure reason had decided upon wearing the gown of jonquil silk that had won Lord Wrexam's approbation. With topaz drops in her ears and a fine Norwich silk shawl draped negligently over her arms at the elbows, she looked far too young and elegant to be attending the ball *en chaperon*, as she was informed, the moment he laid eyes upon her, by the highly eligible baronet she had chosen, from amongst several offers, to gallant them that evening.

This was Sir Mark Thurston, a tall, fresh-faced, good-humoured man who had a very pretty estate in Kent, to which he had showed unmistakable signs of being ready to carry Regina off—once the proper ceremony had been performed, of course, at St. George's, Hanover Square—with quite as good a will as he was showing in escorting her to Almack's. But Regina, though she owned to having spent several very agreeable evenings in his company in Brussels during the winter just past, had up to the present time displayed so little interest in becoming Lady Thurston that Sir Mark, a modest man, had never put his fortune to the touch, and was content this evening to importune her to do no more than stand up with him for a set of country-dances. To this she cordially agreed, but any complacency he might have felt over her prompt assent was at once dashed by her remarking practically that of course her chief business at the ball was not to dance herself but to find partners for Bella, and requesting him to ask her young cousin to stand up with him for the quadrille.

"I shall probably," said Bella, looking out the window at the gas-lit London streets with what she obviously hoped was a very blasé air, "dance the quadrille with Alistair, Sir Mark, but you may have one of the country-dances if you like. Alistair finds country-dances insupportably flat. I hope you do not?"

"Minx!" said Regina, laughing in spite of herself. "If this is the tone you mean to take with all your beaux this evening, it is you who will find the ball insupportably flat, I assure you, for you will be left quite partnerless! Say, 'Thank you,' to Sir Mark for his offer, and that will be quite enough of *Alistair* for tonight." Seeing that Sir Mark was regarding her with a slightly puzzled air, she added, "Alistair, you must know, is Lord Wrexam. Bella made his acquaintance in Ireland this spring, and as he was unwise enough to encourage her to a degree of familiarity, he must now bear the consequences of being Christian-named about London by a schoolroom miss."

"I am *not* a schoolroom miss!" said Bella indignantly. "And Alistair wishes to—" She saw Regina's minatory eye upon her and said rather sulkily, "Oh, very well! But if I can't dance the quadrille with Lord Wrexam, and he hates country-dances, and you have told me all about that perfectly *gothic* custom that I am not permitted to waltz at Almack's until one of the Patronesses has given her approval, when *shall* I be able to dance with him?"

Regina said tranquilly that she was sure she would find she had plenty of partners to make her evening a most successful one, and then suddenly became less tranquil as she saw Sir

Mark's eyes fixed upon her in what seemed rather painful enquiry. That wretched tale of her and Wrexam! she thought, colouring up slightly. No doubt, thanks to Lady Jersey, it had spread all over town by this time. She could not look forward without a slight feeling of trepidation to her meeting with Lord Wrexam that evening.

Once they had arrived in King Street, however, she had no time to consider how his lordship was taking the news that his supposedly violent interest in a young lady he had reason to hold in particular dislike was being bruited about all over town. There were old acquaintances to be greeted, introductions of her young cousin to be made, and engagements to be entered into by both herself and Bella for the evening's dances. Regina, who, as she had told Sir Mark, did not wish to dance a great deal herself, feeling it advisable to be free to give most of her attention to Bella, had just seen her cousin led onto the floor by young Lord Holt, who had fifty thousand a year, estates in Leicestershire and Kent, and a character as blameless as even Lord Arun could have desired, when she found the circle of her own admirers joined by Mr. Lescot, looking more romantically handsome than ever in evening dress, with his dark locks brushed over his forehead in the style known as *au coup de vent*. He promptly asked her to stand up with him for the set that was forming, and looked disappointed when he met with a civil refusal.

"I am dancing very little this evening, you see," she said, "because I must look after Bella—but if you wish to dance with *her*," she added, smiling, "I shall certainly do my best to see to it that you receive a more favourable answer."

Lescot looked slightly uncomfortable. "Believe me, Madame," he said after a moment, "I should be very happy if I thought Lady Arabella would welcome the request. But I fear we—I—"

"You got off quite on the wrong foot together yesterday—is that it?" Regina asked, smiling again. "Never mind; it is quite like Bella to fall into an argument with anyone who has the backbone to stand up to her, but she never holds a grudge. I am sure she will be delighted to dance with you. Do come back and ask her when the set is over."

Lescot, still looking doubtful, said he would, and Regina then enquired how his uncle did.

"He isn't here tonight?" she asked, glancing round the very well-filled Assembly Rooms.

"No," said Lescot. "He wishes to go into society very little, he says. His health, you see, is not robust."

"No, I daresay it is not," Regina said. "He has had a very upsetting life, to be sure. To be obliged to go into exile once is hard enough, but twice—!"

"Yes," agreed Lescot seriously. "It is for that reason, you understand, that I feel myself under obligation to try to smooth his path if I can. He arrived in New Orleans in total destitution, having been accompanied on his voyage from France only by a pair of faithful servants, one of whom, the former agent of his estates, unfortunately died and was buried at sea. All he had been able to save from the debacle in France were some few family keepsakes, which were of great interest to me, of course: they included, for example, a miniature of my mother in her youth—" The young man caught himself up suddenly. "But this is no time to speak of such matters," he said apologetically. "I am keeping you from your friends—"

"Come and meet some of them," Regina suggested kindly, and forthwith made him known to Sir Mark and several other gentlemen, as well as to a very pretty, fair young lady in pink gauze over a white satin slip, whom he at once asked to dance, much to the young lady's satisfaction.

Regina, seeing Bella pass presently from young Lord Holt to an equally eligible young viscount, and then—rather militantly, it seemed to her—to Lescot, while the hands of the clock climbed inexorably towards the hour of eleven, began to hope that Lord Wrexam would not put in an appearance at the ball that evening, after all. Not even for the Duke of Wellington, she was aware, would the Patronesses relax their rule of admitting no one after the stroke of that hour had sounded, and now only five minutes were lacking to it. Three minutes—two—

She was standing looking towards the door, chatting with the Countess Lieven about Switzerland, when she saw that tall, unmistakable figure stroll unhurriedly into the room, quite as if the hands of the clock were not at that moment pointing precisely to the hour. She was unable to conceal a slight start of vexation, and the Countess, looking up quickly, saw Wrexam coming towards them with obvious intent. A mischievous smile appeared quickly upon her face.

"Ah—Wrexam!" she said. "But of course—he comes to *us* first!" She gave her hand to him as he approached. "The magnet draws the iron, I see!" she greeted him, quizzing him with her fine eyes. "The rooms are crowded, but the *eyes of love—*"

"If you could contrive," Wrexam interrupted her, with his usual imperturbable candour, "to behave as charmingly as you look, Madame, one would have nothing more to ask of you." She laughed, quite unoffended and still frankly curious, and made play with her fan as she watched him bow over Regina's hand. "Mrs. Audwyn—" he said to Regina with the same self-composed air, which made her want to hit him, for she was aware that she herself was reacting very markedly to the Countess's scrutiny and colouring up in a most vexatious way. "Since I shall obviously disappoint everyone in the room if I do not ask you to dance with me," continued his lordship, "you may consider yourself asked. Shall we—?"

Regina said rather hurriedly that it was a waltz, and she had best find Bella, who would have to sit it out.

"I shall be delighted to look after your cousin for you," the Countess said promptly, mischief again upon her lovely face. "Since Wrexam has at last made the heroic sacrifice of appearing at one of our balls, surely I owe it to him to see that he is not baulked of his object in doing so!"

She fluttered off forthwith in search of Bella, and Regina found a muscular arm about her waist, sweeping her irresistibly off onto the floor. For perhaps one of the longest minutes she had ever spent in her life she did not look up into Wrexam's face; when she at last did, she found a rather grimly expectant expression upon it.

"Well, Mrs. Audwyn?" he demanded, as her eyes met his.

Spirit flowed back into her at those challenging words.

"After all, it is *your* fault as much as mine," she said. "It wasn't *I* who put the idea into Lady Jersey's head."

"And how was I to know that devilish woman would take the cork-brained notion to fancy there was something between us?" retorted his lordship, now allowing some exasperation to appear in his own tones. "There is no accounting for females! And all because I was trying to oblige you by not publishing my intentions towards Bella—"

Regina looked up at him unbelievingly. "Oh!" she said. "Then you *didn't* speak to her in the same style you used with Lafond—?"

"No, I did not! Good God, didn't I promise you I would do nothing of the sort? This is all Sally's notion of being clever in ferreting out a budding romance before anyone else in town has done so—and I should feel you to be as much a victim of her flight of fancy as I am if I had not learned upon good authority that you did nothing to scotch it when you had the opportunity to do so!"

"Well, you need not look so grim about it!" Regina said, lifting her chin. "After all, there is no great harm done. We have only to behave towards each other with repulsive coldness and the story will die soon enough. I should have thought," she added unkindly, "that you would have known that yourself, and would have realised that practically forcing me to dance with you was *not* the way to accomplish your purpose!"

His lordship looked down at her as if for two pins he would have told her exactly what he thought of malapert females, but restrained himself and in a moment remarked that he was quite willing to behave towards her as repulsively as even she might desire, but that he had considered it wise to discover first whether she perhaps had the intention of acting in exactly the opposite fashion towards him.

"Do you mean, my lord," said Regina, with icy politeness, "that you expected me to fling myself at your head? What a sad disappointment for you, to be sure! Unfortunately, you see, that is a sacrifice of which, even to save Bella from you, I do not find myself capable!"

Unexpectedly, she saw him grin down at her. He had a most engaging smile, she was obliged to admit, which made him seem far less formidable, while at the same time contrarily emphasis-

ing the penetrating keenness of his usually rather lazily veiled
dark eyes.

"*Touché!*" he said. "The coxcomb unmasked. Very well, Mrs.
Audwyn; I shall admit that, as matters stand, you are as much a
victim of circumstances as am I. The question now is—what are
we to do about it? If I may suggest—I am afraid it is usually the
lady who is said to have been snubbed when these promising
affairs are nipped in the bud, unless the gentleman is *galant*
enough to go on showing signs of passion even in the face of
rebuffs. I shall therefore allow *you* to make the first move in
breaking off this exceedingly brief *affaire de coeur,* while I continue to pursue you with my attentions until it becomes quite
clear to all our acquaintances that those attentions are highly unwelcome to you—"

"What an abominable man you are," Regina interrupted
warmly, "putting me quite in the wrong by making me such a
generous offer! And just when I was prepared to dislike you
thoroughly for having pitchforked me into this bumblebath! But
I shall refuse to accept it, of course. We shall *both* be repulsive,
and I shall bear *my* share of the humiliation of being jilted. You
shan't make a martyr of yourself upon *my* account."

"Very well," he said equably. "If you are determined to be
cast off, I shouldn't dream of depriving you of the pleasure. But
since we are committed to dancing the rest of this waltz together, may I suggest that we postpone our mutual repulsiveness
until it has ended—particularly as I should like very much to ask
you if you are acquainted with that revoltingly handsome young
cub who appears to be quarrelling in a particularly intimate way
with Bella over there near the door. He seems to be addressing
her very much in the style of her brother Colin in a frank frater-
nal mood."

Regina glanced around. "Oh, that is Mr. Lescot," she said, "a
connexion of mine in a sort of way. He is a cousin of my late
husband's, and has only just arrived in London from New Orleans. He called upon us yesterday with his uncle, the Comte de
Chelles, and I am afraid he and Bella took each other in instant
dislike."

"Did they, indeed?" said Wrexam thoughtfully, still regarding the handsome young man. "And has he any expectations—this cousin of yours?"

"Expectations? Oh, I should think not, except those that must depend upon his own exertions. Of course he is the Comte de Chelles's nephew, and I believe his heir, which might have counted for a great deal a few years ago; but the Comte, it appears, is quite destitute now. Mr. Lescot is a very agreeable young man, however, and seems to have an excellent understanding, so I daresay he will do very well in the world. Indeed, he is doing so already, for he is the owner of a very considerable plantation in America. But the Comte—the Comte is another matter!"

And to her own immense surprise she found herself confiding to Wrexam the whole story of the Comte's demand upon her for the Chelles necklace, as well as of her discovery of the house in Upper Wimpole Street. And why she should have chosen to tell all this to him, instead of to Sir Mark Thurston or any other well-disposed gentleman of her acquaintance, she could not have said, except that there was something about her tall, broad-shouldered partner that made one instinctively feel that he would know how to deal with problems of any sort and would not hesitate to do so.

The waltz ended as she came to the conclusion of her tale, and Wrexam, remarking at once that he fancied she might care for some lemonade, led her into the refreshment saloon and procured a glass of that innocuous liquid for her. She saw as he handed it to her that he was regarding her with a slight frown, the reason for which suddenly occurred to her.

"If you are wondering," she said obligingly, "whether you ought to tell me that you believe my husband may have leased the house for one of his 'bits of muslin,' as I believe you gentlemen call them, pray feel free to do so—only I shall tell you in advance that I consider you are quite wrong about it. By all I have ever heard, Etienne's 'bits of muslin' were all young women of very expensive tastes, who would have been highly indignant at being offered accommodations in such an unfashionable situation as Upper Wimpole Street. So I am very much afraid you will have to think of some other explanation."

"You are a remarkable young woman, Mrs. Audwyn!" said Wrexam, the glint of a smile now in his eyes. "And I daresay quite right in your assumptions, as well. My acquaintance with your husband was slight, but I *did* know enough of him to be able to confirm your impressions concerning the—er—lighter side of his life. But if it was not for that purpose that he leased this mysterious house, have you any other idea as to why he may have wished to do so?"

"None at all," confessed Regina. "You see, Etienne never talked to me about things. As a matter of fact, we scarcely ever saw each other, so he couldn't."

"I see. *Not* an ideal marriage," Wrexam said dryly. "Now I remember, Arun hinted as much."

"Well, it doesn't matter *now*," Regina said quickly. "Only it *does* rather leave me without a clue. And why Baker? It sounds very sinister, for some reason. I have the most uncomfortable feeling that I shall go to Upper Wimpole Street and find the house like Bluebeard's Castle, with corpses in every room; only Etienne wasn't like that, *really*. For instance, I can see how he might have *wished* to commit murder when he found himself leg-shackled to a schoolgirl he didn't care for in the least, with *no* conversation and high expectations of storybook romance; but he didn't. He simply went away and ignored me. Which rather proves he was essentially peaceable—doesn't it?"

"A *very* remarkable young woman," Wrexam repeated, the glinting smile now quite pronounced in his eyes. "But I feel you wrong yourself, Mrs. Audwyn. You can never have been entirely without conversation. About the house, though—your solicitor, it appears, is likely to be of very little use to you. Is there anyone else—?"

"Well, there is Uncle Ned's solicitor, Mr. Pipping," Regina said doubtfully. "He is very good about finding proper servants and dealing with upholsterers who say they can't possibly have the sofa finished in time, but I expect he would be dreadfully shocked about an affair like this, particularly if it turns out that Etienne *was* up to something really havey-cavey. And I daresay he might turn awfully *legal* about the necklace, if I *do* find it, and insist upon taking steps about it in the Court of Chancery or whatever it is, when all I really want to do is to turn it over to the Comte at once, because he seems to be horridly poor now and quite dependent upon Mr. Lescot's charity. So I shall certainly not tell Mr. Pipping anything about it unless I must."

"You are quite sure," Wrexam enquired, after a moment's pause, "that the necklace rightfully *is* the property of the Comte de Chelles? It would appear, by his description, to be an extremely valuable piece."

Regina stared at him. "But of course it is his property!" she said. "Whose else should it be? It was certainly not Etienne's, or he would have gamed it away, even if it *was* a family heirloom."

She suddenly became aware that Lady Jersey had come into the refreshment saloon and had fixed an interested gaze upon her and Wrexam, and instantly the oddity of her speaking in this intimate way to a man with whom the only business she wished to have was to discourage his attentions to Bella overcame her. She coloured up in vexation and fell silent.

"*Now* what is the matter?" Wrexam demanded, in his usual abrupt manner. He glanced round, saw Lady Jersey regarding them, and shrugged his shoulders. "I see!" he said. "It is time for you to resume your *repulsive* tactics. May I ask, then, that you allow me to continue this conversation with you later in the privacy of Cavendish Square, where neither Sally Jersey nor any other of the town's tattlemongers need know of it? I have the feeling that there is something more in it than meets the eye, and I should rather you do nothing at all about it until we are able to discuss it further."

It was perhaps fortunate, Regina thought, as she left the refreshment saloon upon Wrexam's arm, that his lordship's autocratic habit of command left him with no doubt in his mind of her complying with his directives, as she did not wish to quarrel with him again in public and yet had not the least intention of discussing her affairs with him any further. She had, in fact, she told herself in vexation, been very unwise to have confided in him at all. Upon their return to the ballroom, she behaved towards him with such compensatory coolness that he complimented her gravely and said he was sure he would be credited with nursing a broken heart if only he, in turn, would play his part by retiring to prop one of the walls of the ballroom and following her with jealous eyes for the remainder of the evening.

"Which unfortunately I can't, because I must dance with Bella," he said. "I wonder what she is making of all this very peculiar gossip that is going round about us? But then one need never worry about Bella. She is so splendidly insensitive; I can't imagine her having a fit of the vapours, no matter what odd tales she might hear about me."

And he took himself off to find his young inamorata, whom Regina soon saw standing up with him very happily for a set of the despised country-dances. It was quite true, as Wrexam had said, she thought, that her young cousin was impervious to shock, or else she had somehow managed to escape the rumour that seemed to have reached the ears of almost everyone else in the Assembly Rooms.

But that it had indeed reached Bella's ears was made perfectly clear to Regina after they had returned to Cavendish Square that night. She and Bella, the latter perched in her night-dress upon Regina's bed as her cousin brushed her hair before the dressing-table mirror, were discussing Bella's very satisfactory conquests of the evening, among them that of young Lord Holt, which seemed to have been complete, for he had stood up with her for two dances and had begged for a third, reluctantly denied by Regina on the grounds of propriety.

"Not," said Bella, "that it matters, at any rate, because of course I am going to marry Alistair," and then, without pausing to draw breath, dropped her bombshell. "What," she demanded, "do you think the Countess Lieven said to me about Alistair this evening as I was sitting beside her during one of the waltzes?"

Regina, looking guilty, said she had not the least idea.

"She asked me," Bella said, "how I should like having him for a cousin-in-law. And when I stared and asked her what she could mean, she said I must know that it was only to see *you* that he had come to Almack's this evening! Of course I could scarcely keep from laughing! I began to say she was *quite* out, and that you disliked each other excessively; but then I thought what a good joke it would be to let her go on thinking it and perhaps even spread the tale about, and how diverted Alistair will be when he hears of it!"

She looked at Regina as if anticipating her joining in her appreciation of the jest, but for some reason her cousin seemed not to find it amusing. She was frowning over a tangle in her curls, pulled at it so hard that her eyes watered, and suggested rather abruptly that Bella go off to bed.

"Oh, very well," said Bella tolerantly, getting up. "I expect you are tired. But I do really wish Alistair hadn't taken you so much in dislike, and you him. It will make things so very uncomfortable when I am married to him."

And, with an enormous yawn, she went off to her own bedchamber, leaving Regina to toss and turn in a most unprecedented way for a very long time upon her own pillow. It was utterly incomprehensible, she thought as she did so, how, no matter how she tried to keep Wrexam out of Bella's life and her own, he seemed always to be coming back into it, an imperturbable and quite immovable obstacle to everything she had hoped to accomplish during this Season.

Only this time, she told herself in conscience-stricken candour, it was no one's fault but her own, for was it not she who had encouraged Lady Jersey to believe that the idea she had taken into her head about Wrexam's *tendre* for her was true, and, likewise, was it not she who had confided to Wrexam her difficulties over the Chelles diamonds?

But she would turn over a new leaf from this time forward, she decided firmly; indeed, if she did not, she thought, with a sudden very peculiar feeling inside her, almost anything might happen, though what she meant by "almost anything" she did not bother or perhaps was too cowardly to define. But, at any rate, it was with a fixed determination ruthlessly to cut off any further communication with Lord Wrexam beyond that demanded by the merest civility that she at last fell asleep that night.

CHAPTER

The first thing necessary to carry this praiseworthy resolution into effect was, she decided the next morning, to go at once to see the house in Upper Wimpole Street and thus forestall any attempt by Wrexam to take a further part in that business. Colin, approached upon the subject at the breakfast table, magnanimously declared himself willing to forgo a look-in at Tattersall's in the company of his new boon companion, the erstwhile Harrovian, Mr. Crowcroft, to accompany her there, and they accordingly set off together a short time later, having sternly repressed a mutiny in the nursery ranks that had had the object of enlarging their party to include Maria and Giles as well. It was bad enough, Regina thought, to be exposing a youth of Colin's tender years to whatever unseemly mysteries were to be found in Upper Wimpole Street, without bringing along the nursery contingent as well.

The house in Upper Wimpole Street, when she and Colin arrived there, turned out to be a good Georgian structure, three stories high, with a restrained expression and a prim doorway, of the kind that might be seen in dozens of other streets all over London. There was a cheerful-looking young man running down the steps of its neighbour to the right and a stout nurse with two small children in charge just arriving at its neighbour to the left; the only remarkable thing about it was the fact that the blinds of its well-proportioned sash windows were all tightly drawn. But in spite of its deserted appearance, Regina had an odd impression, as she took the key from her reticule and gave it to Colin, that they were being observed from inside, and that Colin, too, had something of the same feeling she gathered from the sudden sharp glance she saw him cast at one of the upper windows.

All he said, however, was, "Rum sort of place," as he set the key in the lock and turned it; and the next moment they stepped inside into the narrow hall.

It seemed, in the dim light, to be quite unfurnished, and showed them only a pair of doors opening at one side, with a steep staircase at the far end leading to an upper storey. A pervading musty, unused air at once struck them disagreeably. As they paused together in the hall, Colin for once looking rather uncertain, Regina was conscious of a strong desire simply to turn around and walk out of this stale, silent dimness into the bright morning sunlight; but the thought of the Chelles diamonds deterred her and, taking herself in hand, she said bracingly to Colin, "We'll open some windows. Goodness! How dark it is! Shall we try this room first?"

She trod across the hall to the first door, which stood half open, and walked inside. To her surprise, it appeared, like the hall, to be quite bare of furniture; there was not even a carpet upon the floor. Only at the windows there were heavy draperies, which turned out to be red when Colin had flung them aside and let the light in.

"Well!" said Colin, gazing about rather blankly at the four bare walls of the room. "I was right about one thing, anyway. Etienne didn't keep another wife here. Unless she absconded with all the furniture—"

"Well, *someone* has absconded with it," Regina said. "Or perhaps there never was any. Only if there wasn't—what on earth was Etienne doing with this place?" She started as a sudden stealthy sound made itself heard in the silence. "What was that?" she enquired a trifle nervously.

"Rats, probably," said Colin, with admirable nonchalance. "Bound to be some about, with no one living here. It came from upstairs, didn't it? Shall I go up and see?"

"We'll both go," Regina said, wishing she did not feel it necessary to sound so cheerful and unconcerned. "But of course there can be no one here. The door was locked, and the windows certainly must be, too."

"Well, there doesn't seem to be anything to steal, so I don't see why anyone should trouble to break in," Colin agreed, following her out into the hall once more and glancing through the open door of the second room as they walked past it. "This one's empty, too. Are you quite sure Etienne wasn't a bit queer in his attic, Reggie? I mean to say, you hear of people—"

"Well, I certainly have never heard of anyone who leased an empty house for years for no reason whatsoever!" Regina said. "And it isn't in the least like Etienne to have done such a thing. What *can* he have been doing here?"

"Counterfeiting?" suggested Colin, following her as she began cautiously mounting the dark stairs.

"Don't be absurd! Etienne wasn't a criminal. Besides, he never had any money."

"Well—smuggling, then."

"In Upper Wimpole Street?"

"Perhaps he just wanted a place to hide the diamonds."

"I am beginning to doubt very seriously that there *are* any diamonds. The whole affair seems completely mad to me, and I have a good notion to walk straight out of here, give the key back to Mr. Copplestone, and forget that Upper Wimpole Street exists—*Oh!*" With the exclamation, she halted abruptly at the threshold of a room opening at the head of the staircase. "*That,*" she said, in a lowered voice of extreme conviction, "was *not* rats!"

She clutched Colin's arm, and for once that imperturbable young gentleman was shocked into silence as well. There had certainly been a series of sounds from below that no rat, or army of rats, was capable of making—the sound of the opening of a door, and then that of leisurely footsteps upon an uncarpeted floor. As Regina and Colin listened, still without speaking and almost without breathing, the footsteps began unhurriedly to mount the stairs.

"What shall we *do?*" whispered Regina.

She felt Colin's arm tighten protectively, albeit somewhat

nervously, about her—and then suddenly a familiar dark head, followed by a pair of broad shoulders in an impeccably tailored corbeau-coloured coat, rose into view in the dim stairwell, and Wrexam's voice remarked calmly, "I rather thought I should find you up here. The lower floor seemed to be quite deserted."

"Wrexam!" exclaimed Regina, her apprehension giving way to indignation on the moment. "What are *you* doing here? Do you know you have frightened us half out of our wits?"

"No, have I? I'm sorry—but if you don't care to invite intruders, you shouldn't leave the door on the latch, you know." He glanced into the darkened room before the door of which she stood, murmured an apology, and, walking past her into it, flung up the blinds. Again the morning sunlight fell brightly upon a bare, dusty floor and four bare walls. "I must say, your late husband had a rather odd taste in house furnishings," remarked Wrexam, looking at the cold grate, where a few half-burned scraps of what appeared to be newspapers remained as the only evidence of former human habitation. "Simplicity carried to a rather Spartan extreme—don't you agree?"

He strolled over, picked up the charred scraps from the grate and examined them. "The *Morning Post*—March 18, 1814," he read. "The Earl of Morran announces the betrothal of his only daughter, the Lady Amelia Melicent Sedbury, to Sir Henry Chesham, Bart., of Chesham Hall, Herts., the wedding to take place on the 29th instant, at St. Martin's Church, Almanderly, Leicester. . . ." The second scrap, likewise from the *Morning Post,* announced the marriage of the Honourable Miss Maria Banks, of Bracken Hill, Bucks., to Sir Barnaby Aberfoyle. "Did your husband perhaps take a violent interest in marriages among the *ton?*" he enquired politely, raising his eyes to meet Regina's still fulminating ones.

"No, of course he did not!" she said. "And you *haven't* answered my question. What are you doing here? And how did you know where I was?"

"That is two questions—but never mind, I shall answer them both," said Wrexam. "I knew you were here because Bella told me—by the bye, you should be exceedingly grateful to me for not bringing her, too, along with your other young cousins, who were mightily set upon accompanying me—and what I am doing here is trying to assist you in finding the Chelles diamonds. You have not come across them as yet, I collect?"

"No, I have not! The house, as you have seen for yourself, is quite empty."

"Ah, but, do you know, I have the oddest feeling that it is not!" Wrexam said; and, to her astonishment, he suddenly strode across the room to where she was standing in the doorway and, putting her aside rather abruptly, walked out of the room. The next moment she heard him running down the stairs.

"What in heaven's name—!" she began, to Colin.

But Colin, deserting her as hastily as Wrexam had done, was already bolting for the stairs. She heard him clattering down them, taking two or three at a time by the sound of it, and then his voice calling rather breathlessly to Wrexam.

"I say, sir! What's up? Was there someone—?"

"Yes. I've lost him, worse luck. A young, active fellow with black hair. I had only a glimpse of him as he pelted off round the corner."

"Shan't we go after him?"

"My dear Colin, one can't go about pursuing a perfect stranger in the street and then calling for a constable to take him up because one alleges he may have been without permission in a house one does not own."

"But—"

"Don't fret yourself. I am quite sure we shall have an opportunity at some future date to come to grips with him."

By this time Regina had also descended the stairs, and was surveying the two with a rather perturbed but militant air.

"Oh no, you will not!" she said to Wrexam. "Colin is coming back with me at once to Cavendish Square, and I shall lock up this odious house and give the key back to Mr. Copplestone. If there is nothing inside it but housebreakers, I do not see what possible good we can do by coming here again!"

Colin looked at her reproachfully. "Oh, come, Reggie!" he urged. "It's not like you to be so poor-spirited! Surely you can't wish to leave before we've searched the house! After all, we haven't even seen the attics, or the cellar—"

"And I don't wish to see them," Regina said firmly.

"Mrs. Audwyn is quite right," Wrexam interposed. He turned to her soothingly. "It will be far better for you to return to Cavendish Square at once," he said. "Colin and I will join you there after we have conducted a thorough search of the premises. You may leave the key with us—"

"I shall do nothing of the sort!" said Regina indignantly. "This is *not* your affair, Lord Wrexam!"

"Come, come—you forget that I am soon to be a member of the family!" Wrexam reminded her reprovingly. He held out his hand. "May I have the key?"

"No!" said Regina. "If you are determined to search this revolting place, I shall stay, too. Only I *shan't* go into the cellar! Heaven knows what you will find there—another housebreaker, or perhaps even a skeleton!"

Colin, who appeared to find both these alternatives equally inviting, said magnanimously that if they did find a skeleton he would come up straight away to tell her so that she could see it, too, but Wrexam remarked rather dampingly that if there were any skeletons they would probably only be those of rats.

"Why," he suggested to Regina, "don't you remain here while Colin and I explore the cellar, Mrs. Audwyn? You might employ the time profitably in looking to see if there are any likely places for secret panels or anything of the sort"—which romantic suggestion made Colin's eyes light up with pure joy, but caused Regina to look at him blightingly. She was not Bella, she thought, to be treated as a child and amused with fancies—but when she had been left alone in the empty, echoing room, for some reason the idea of a secret panel seemed to become rather less fanciful, and she occupied herself for a time very earnestly in a thoughtful survey of all the walls on the ground floor, which were unfortunately papered over in patterns of varying degrees of hideousness, offering no proper scope at all to a manufacturer of secret panels.

Exploration of the large and ornate chimney pieces in the rooms that had apparently served as drawing room and dining room turned out to be equally unrewarding. Both were of heavily carved and gilded wood in the pseudo-Gothic style, the one in the drawing room being upheld by a pair of rather squashed-looking caryatids representing Paris and Venus, depicted with very large heads and rather rudimentary limbs, the former in the act of presenting the golden apple to the simpering goddess facing him across the yawning hearth. Beyond the possibility that the caryatids had been built hollow for the purpose of providing a convenient hiding place for such unlikely baubles as diamond necklaces, however, neither this piece of domestic architecture nor its companion in the dining room appeared to offer any possibilities of concealment except if one explored inside the chimney itself. But Regina had no intention of doing so, inspired both by concern for her elegant sea-green walking dress and by a vague and quite unscientific conviction that the diamonds would have melted up there if anyone had been thoughtless enough to have built a fire beneath them.

She was examining the dusty red draperies at the drawing-room windows, as far up as she could reach them without standing upon a chair, of which there was none available, when Wrexam and Colin came up from the cellar to report an open window, through which the housebreaker had probably entered, but nothing else that was not covered at least an inch thick in dust and cobwebs, so that it obviously predated the period during which Etienne had had the house.

"And no skeletons, either rat or human, you will be happy to hear," Wrexam said, "but plenty of black beetles. On the whole, a most unattractive and quite unhelpful place, I am afraid." He glanced at her hands, which had been made very grimy by the red curtains, informed her kindly that there was a smut upon her forehead, and remarked, "I gather your search has been quite as unrewarding as ours?"

"Yes, but there are still the attics," Colin, whose hunting blood was up, put in with unabated enthusiasm. "I'll bet you anything you like we shall find something there. Do come along, Reggie!"

And he bounded out into the hall and up the stairs. Wrexam's hand upon her arm prevented Regina from following him.

"Would you mind waiting for just a moment?" he asked. "There is a question I'd like to put to you while Colin is out of the way." She looked at him in rather puzzled enquiry, for his manner was slightly more serious than was usual, but before she could speak he went on at once, "It concerns your late husband. Could you tell me what his political leanings were?"

"His political leanings?" Regina's puzzlement deepened to astonishment. "But what on earth can they have to say to anything?"

"Perhaps nothing—perhaps a great deal," Wrexam said. "Do you know, for example, where his sympathies lay in the late war?"

"His sympathies? But—but with England, of course!"

"You are quite certain of that? He was half French, I understand."

"Yes," said Regina. "His mother was the Comte de Chelles's sister. But his father was English, and Etienne himself lived in England almost all his life. Surely you can't believe that he—"

"As a meeting-place for persons engaged in certain clandestine activities during the late war, this house might have been distinctly useful, you know," Wrexam remarked reflectively. "The eccentric Mr. Baker, who paid down his rent so promptly but was seldom to be seen in Upper Wimpole Street, might have received his visitors in these ostentatiously respectable surroundings without attracting the least attention from the authorities—"

"But what reason can you possibly have for thinking such a thing?" Regina demanded, feeling remarkably confused as she tried to fit the picture of her elegant, rakish husband into this suddenly suggested role of conspirator. "It is—it must be quite absurd!"

"Is it?" Wrexam drew from his pocket the charred scraps of paper he had removed from the grate of the bedroom upstairs and handed them to her. "If you will observe," he said, "you will see that some of the letters in these notices are faintly underlined—"

Regina did as she was told, and, with some of the surprised self-satisfaction one feels when a puzzle comes out right, spelled out slowly, "M-o-n-d-a-y. 9 a.m. C-a-l-a-i- Calais?" she finished it for herself as the message broke off, owing to the paper's having been burnt away at that spot.

"I should think so," Wrexam said. "Rather childish, of course—

but then I daresay one is quite out in believing that spies are universally devilishly clever people. Quite ordinary, most of them, I expect."

"But does it—? No, it *can't* mean that Etienne was—was involved with French agents!" Regina expostulated, her brain reeling as she tried to cope with this amazing idea. "There must be some other explanation! Etienne simply *wasn't* that sort of man." She tried to explain, rather helplessly, "He wasn't in the least interested in politics, or the war, or—or anything of that sort. He only cared about horses, and gaming, and—"

"And women?" Wrexam finished it for her. "I daresay you may be right—but one does sometimes surprise even oneself by the odd things one decides to do, you know. And there *was* the element of risk in the thing—something that's bound to appeal to a gaming man. Lord knows, there are a dozen ways he might have been drawn into it—perhaps even through Chelles himself. I understand the Comte did very well for himself under Bonaparte, and had a rather large stake in his remaining in power."

"Well," Regina admitted, "he—I mean the Comte—*did* know about this house, when no one else did; that is certainly true. He *said* he had made enquiries, but he couldn't have done if he hadn't known what to make enquiries *about*, if one really comes to think of it."

"Exactly," said Wrexam. "I am rather afraid, you know, that there may be more to all this than meets the eye. Perhaps you had best wait until I can make some enquiries on my own account before you do anything further in this business."

Regina began to say that this seemed sensible to her, because in the first place there was nothing further that she *could* do, since she hadn't found the necklace and didn't know where else to look for it; but then she caught herself up sharply. What *was* there, she thought, about this insidious man that continually made her forget that the only business she properly had with him was to see to it that he did not marry Bella? It was certainly not his conciliating manners, because he appeared to take no pains at all to conciliate her or even not to be rude to her whenever it suited him to be; but he had a way of calmly taking it for granted that one was going to confide one's difficulties to him that caught one off one's guard now and then most unfairly.

But she was not off her guard now, so she said in a tone that she tried to make very cool and final that it was kind of him to take an interest in the matter, but she was sure she would manage very well without him.

"No, you won't," said Wrexam bluntly. "You'll make a deuced mull of it. But we shan't quarrel about it. I'll go my way and you go yours, and we shall see which of us comes out with the right answer. Are you angry with me for suggesting that your husband may have been involved in Bonapartist intrigues?" he asked abruptly.

"No—only bewildered," Regina said slowly. "You see, I already knew he was not a—an admirable man. Only I still can't think you are right in believing that he—" She broke off suddenly in vexation, exclaiming, "Now you have me doing it again!"

"Doing what?"

"Confiding in you. If you weren't always so abominably blunt-spoken, and were oily and unctuous instead, I might be able to remember that you are really a blackhearted schemer, intent on worming your way into my good graces so you may see more of Bella—"

"Oh, I can see quite as much of Bella as I care to," Wrexam said confidently. "There is no way you can prevent it unless you stop doing the Season with her and shut her up in Cavendish Square—which I *don't* advise, as she has come up with some peculiar ideas about rope-ladder elopements in the dead of night that I am afraid Arun wouldn't care for at all."

Regina turned pale. "Rope-ladder elopements!" she said. "You *wouldn't!*"

"No, *I* wouldn't," Wrexam agreed. "When I step into Parson's mouse-trap I intend to do it with all proper pomp and ceremony at St. George's, Hanover Square, so as to impress upon myself what is expected of me in future. But I can't answer for Bella; if I don't co-operate, she may look around for some other willing victim. Where *do* girls pick up these extraordinarily silly ideas? You may raise them in the country for seventeen years, but let them loose in a London lending-library for two afternoons together and they catch romanticism as if it were a disease!"

"Well, of course Bella is romantic!" Regina said, with spirit. "All girls are—and most boys, too, in their time. I expect if you were to look back, you would find that you were quite as intrigued by the idea of rope-ladders in your grasstime as Bella is now—unless you were born as cynical and cold-blooded as you are today, which I shouldn't be surprised to hear, either!"

"Oh, no!" said Wrexam coolly. "I shouldn't think that description would have fitted me in the least. In point of fact, I daresay I committed more than my share of follies when I was a halfling, but they never, I am happy to say, included eloping with anyone, *via* rope-ladder or any other route. So if it will relieve your mind, I can promise you that it is highly unlikely Bella will find me a willing accomplice in such a venture. Only think what a figure I should cut if I were discovered by the watch at two in the morning in Cavendish Square, assisting a young female out of a second-storey window! I should never dare show my face in White's again!"

At which Regina was obliged to laugh and to say she was glad his dislike of committing a social solecism, if not his conscience, would prevent him from carrying Bella off to Gretna. Then Colin came down to report that the attics appeared no more promising than the cellar, containing nothing except a few sticks of broken furniture that had obviously been there since the Flood, and by mutual agreement the house was locked up again and they all went away.

CHAPTER
9

On the following day Sir Mark Thurston had engaged himself to drive Regina and Bella to Hampton Court, with Maria and Giles being allowed to accompany them as a special treat. It was one of the things that Regina liked best about Sir Mark that he was always willing to endure with equanimity not only Colin's attacks of extreme man-of-the-town sophistication, but also the onslaughts upon his person of Maria and Giles, who had immediately adopted him as a kind of vice-uncle and behaved towards him with uninhibited and sometimes embarrassing Stacpoole affection.

"He is without doubt one of the nicest men I have ever known," she was obliged to admit to herself, on the morning after her visit to Upper Wimpole Street, "and if I had the least degree of sense I should allow him to come to the point, as he is obviously longing to do, and then marry him at once. Only I shan't," she completed the thought, not without a certain feeling of exasperation towards herself for being so foolish; and she set herself determinedly to the task of going through her morning mail, which was very large that day, owing to the arrival of a great many acceptances responding to the cards of invitation that had been sent out for the ball to be given the following week in Bella's honour.

She was interrupted presently by the advent of a somewhat unwelcome caller, the Comte de Chelles. She had been racking her brains since the previous day as to how to deal with the matter of the Comte and the missing necklace, for he obviously did not believe she knew nothing about it and she could not think how she was to convince him that there was no possible way in which she could help him to recover it.

She was relieved, however, to see him come in with the same rather unctuous air of amiability that she remembered from his last visit, and during the exchange of civilities that followed she had time to hope that perhaps he really was a little mad and had only invented the necklace, and would have forgotten all about it by this time.

But these hopes were quickly dashed as the Comte, leaning forward and bending upon her the rather unnervingly penetrating stare of his black eyes, suddenly enquired, "And the necklace, *chère Madame?* The Chelles diamonds? You have now discovered them—*hein?*"

"Discovered them? No, I'm afraid I haven't," said Regina, a trifle nervously under that unmoving stare. "If I had, I should have given them to you at once, of course."

"Ah!" The Comte uttered the monosyllable on a long, significant breath, his eyes continuing to bore into her face. "You have *not* found them? But you have, I believe, found the house in Upper Wimpole Street—*c'est vrai, n'est-ce pas?*"

"Well, yes. I've found *that,* but I assure you, there are no diamonds there, Comte," Regina said. "In fact, it is quite empty, and I can't think why Etienne can have wished to rent it. It is all the greatest puzzle to me—"

"Aha!" said the Comte, varying the exclamation but continuing to stare at her so perseveringly that Regina found herself wondering if she was wrong in reading menace in that stare. "It is a puzzle to you, is it?" he said. "And it is a puzzle to *me, chère Madame,*" he went on, with marked emphasis, "how you can know nothing of this so important matter, upon which—*ça se voit!*—my entire future depends. I am now, as you see, a poor man, Madame; my fortune is all—how do you say it?—*volée,* robbed from me by this new regime. To part with an heirloom that has been in the hands of my family since the days of François Premier will be of the highest repugnance to me, but when

I recover the necklace I must steel myself: these diamonds, I tell myself, will be to me the bread in my mouth, the roof above my head. But you, Madame, *une jolie femme, jeune,* with every opportunity to arrange your own life so that you may live in comfort, perhaps even luxury—*you* would deny me that bread, that roof—"

"But I am not denying you anything!" Regina protested. "I *don't* have the diamonds and I haven't the least notion where to look for them. My cousin and I thoroughly searched the house in Upper Wimpole Street yesterday, but we certainly found no diamond necklace—" She broke off, paling slightly as she was struck by a sudden thought. "Good heavens!" she said. "Can it be possible—?" She looked rather agitatedly at the Comte. "There *was* someone else in the house when my cousin and I were there yesterday," she said. "It never occurred to us at the time that it wasn't a mere housebreaker—but perhaps it *might* have been someone who knew that the diamonds were there and had come on purpose to steal them—"

The Comte pounced upon her before she could go any further.

"Someone in the house?" he demanded. "You saw him—this intruder? You can describe him?"

"Well, no, *I* can't," Regina said, "but Lord Wrexam, who was there as well and helped us to search the house, caught a glimpse of him as he ran out, and he says he was a young, active man with black hair." Her puzzlement returned. "But if he *wasn't* merely a housebreaker, and had come on purpose to steal the diamonds, how did he learn they were there?" she said. "If they *were* there, they had apparently lain there in perfect safety for years—yet now, suddenly, just when you have come in search of them— You have told no one else about the house and the necklace, have you?"

"No one but yourself, Madame," said the Comte impressively. "Except, of course—Gervais."

"Gervais? Mr. Lescot? But you *can't* suspect *him*—!"

The Comte shook his head sadly. "Alas, Madame," he said, "when one has passed through as many evils in life as *I* have, one learns to trust no one! Gervais has behaved nobly towards me in my difficulties, but still he is, *vous savez,* a young man with his way to make in life, and young men are sometimes impatient. But I will say nothing, *moi!* No—except that he is young and active, and has hair of a blackness—"

Regina shook her head and said she really could not believe that Mr. Lescot, who seemed so pleasant and unassuming and quite reliable, for all his romantic good looks, would do such a thing. But in spite of herself she could not forget that horrid little seed of suspicion that the Comte had planted in her mind, and after he had gone she remembered that he had mentioned, on the occasion of his first morning-call, how quickly Lescot had decided that he, too, wished to visit England and the Continent when the Comte had broached the matter of his returning there to salvage what he could of his lost fortune. Personable and agreeable young men, she reminded herself unhappily, had been known before this to have betrayed the trust of unsuspecting persons in order to lay their hands upon far smaller amounts of money than the Chelles diamonds would seem to be worth.

The arrival of Lescot himself in Cavendish Square hot on the heels of his uncle's departure did little to quiet the doubts concerning him that had been raised by the Comte. Colin had come into the drawing room by that time, full of the plan he had conceived of making a further search that afternoon of the house in Upper Wimpole Street, which would include sounding the walls for the detection of secret passages and examining the floors for the presence of trap-doors, and it seemed to Regina that Lescot displayed a distinct and even somewhat inordinate interest in the matter.

"Why don't you come with me?" Colin, also conscious of that interest, at last invited him generously; but Lescot said regretfully that, as his trip to England combined business and pleasure and he had an appointment for the afternoon that came under the former heading, he would be obliged to decline.

"I only came in for a moment to ask if Lady Arabella would care to drive to the Botanical Gardens with me tomorrow," he said, his dark, handsome face flushing up slightly. "That is, if you have no objection, Mrs. Audwyn? If she's not too busy, I wonder if I might see her for a moment and ask her—"

Regina said of course he might see her, and rang for Hughes

to have a message carried upstairs to her. She then wished she had said at once that Bella had another engagement, for it certainly would not do to wean her young cousin away from her infatuation with Wrexam only to fling her into the arms of a young man of whom one really knew nothing at all, and who might even be a completely unscrupulous adventurer, in spite of his noble birth.

But Bella saved her the trouble of worrying about it by coming into the drawing room with an air of having been dragged there much against her will, listening with distinct impatience to young Mr. Lescot's rather stammering invitation, and then stating curtly that she would be far too much occupied on the morrow to go to the Botanical Gardens or anywhere else with him.

"I see," said Lescot, looking rather daunted. "Then perhaps the following day—?"

"I don't see why I should go anywhere at all with you," Bella said severely. "You only quarrel with me when we are together."

Lescot, his brows beginning to lower like those of any young man of spirit who realises that he is being baited, said he was exceedingly sorry if she felt like that, but if it was not ungentlemanly for him to say so, she did her share of the quarrelling.

"Well, it *is* ungentlemanly," Bella declared, and then, having stared him entirely out of countenance, did a complete volte-face with the unpredictability of her sex and suddenly said graciously, "Oh, very well! Tomorrow, then, you may call for me at three."

Lescot, looking a trifle stunned by this reversal, thanked her and went away, upon which Bella remarked that she couldn't think why she had said she would go with him, because he was the most disagreeable person she had ever met.

"Well, perhaps you can find some excuse to put him off," Regina said, conscious of inculcating very poor manners but still worried about the suitability of Lescot as a replacement for Wrexam.

But Bella said she didn't think she would, because she would like to visit the Botanical Gardens, and perhaps they might stop and see the Tower and some of the other popular London sights as well, because Alistair found that sort of thing a dead bore and she would never see them if she waited for him to take her.

So Regina, cheered by the thought that at least Bella was beginning to discover a certain incompatibility between her own and her lover's tastes, went back to her letters, and soon afterwards, prompt to his time, Sir Mark arrived to escort them to Hampton Court.

Sir Mark had brought the smart yellow-bodied barouche in which, as a member of the famous Four-Horse Club, he was accustomed to drive to Salt Hill on the first and third Thursdays of May and June, much to the admiration and envy of all the aspiring whips in town who had not been invited to join this august assemblage. Giles at once demanded, and received, the right to sit on the box beside him, and when the other members of the party had been comfortably accommodated the horses were set in motion and the barouche moved off.

Almost at once, to everyone's surprise, there was a clatter of hooves behind them and Lord Wrexam, on a neatish bay, drew up beside the barouche and set his horse to an accommodating trot beside it.

"Good morning!" he said calmly. "I very nearly missed you, didn't I? That would have been rather a pity!"

Regina, conscious of Sir Mark's enquiring and rather rigidly polite gaze upon him, said to Bella in a hasty undertone, "Did *you* ask him to come?"

"Oh, no!" said Bella, who was looking pleased and preening herself a little. "I only told him where we were going. I expect he couldn't keep away." She raised her voice and said to Wrexam, above the steady clatter of the horses' hooves, "Are you really coming with us? How splendid! You know Sir Mark Thurston, don't you?"

"Oh, yes," said Wrexam, greeting Sir Mark with equanimity. "We're both members of the F.H.C." He went on, to Sir Mark, "I expect you'll be very grateful to me before the day is out for having joined the party, Thurston. Two ladies and a pair of the most egregious brats ever to come out of Ireland is a bit much for any man, I think you'll find; and I can at least take Bella off your hands."

Sir Mark, brightening considerably at the conclusion of this speech, said of course they would be glad of Wrexam's company, and then devoted his attention once more to his horses as Wrexam held his own bay beside the carriage and inaugurated a conversation with Bella. Regina, who had by this time got herself in hand, contented herself with looking disapproving, and was just as well pleased as not that Maria, jealous of Giles's place upon the box beside Sir Mark, made up for the dulness of being obliged to sit tamely on a proper seat by demanding, and getting, most of Wrexam's attention.

In this way they arrived at last at the spot in the enchanting Thames countryside where the river made its gentle loop through the green watermeadows of Hampton Court, and the mellow red Tudor brick work of the Palace came into view. Regina, who had visited it several times before and had already had the pleasure of becoming lost in its famous Maze, would have preferred, on this perfect day in May, to wander through the gardens, now brilliant with spring flowers, rather than enjoy the frustration of being unable to find her way out of the endless green alleys of that fascinating labyrinth. But Maria and Giles clamoured to enter it at once, and as she did not trust Bella to keep a proper eye upon them, with Wrexam in the company, she resigned herself to accompanying them. Sir Mark would have joined them, but she had no idea of allowing Wrexam an hour's uninterrupted tête-à-tête with Bella, so when he had purchased their tickets she said to him, "You will be bored to extinction if you come with us; do go and join Bella and Lord Wrexam instead. I believe they are going into the gardens."

Sir Mark looked disappointed and, for a good-humoured man, rather stubborn.

"But I had much rather go with you," he said.

"Yes, I know, but you can't," said Regina decidedly. "Bella won't go into the Maze without Lord Wrexam, and *he* will certainly not do so while he can talk to her alone! Surely you can see the impropriety of my leaving them together!"

Sir Mark looked as if he would have liked to damn Lord Wrexam and all his works, but being a reasonable man he was obliged to admit that she was right, and went off rather unhappily to join the others.

A half hour passed. Giles and Maria were lost, individually and in company, upon three occasions, requiring a great deal of hallooing and appeals to the custodian, whose stand commanded a view of the entire labyrinth, to bring them all together again, and Regina was beginning to grow hot and a little tired when she was suddenly startled to see Sir Mark approaching her down one of the green alleys.

"Oh!" she said accusingly. "I thought you were going to stay with the others!"

"So I was," said Sir Mark, who was also, she now saw, looking hot and rather vexed. "But Lady Arabella and Wrexam decided *they* would come in, so I was obliged to accompany them. Only Lady Arabella ran off—in jest, of course—and when Wrexam and I began looking for her, *we* became separated, too—"

"Yes, I daresay you did!" said Regina rather unkindly. "And he is no doubt now enjoying a delightful tête-à-tête with her in one of these cul-de-sacs! Really, Sir Mark, how could you allow them to diddle you so easily?"

"Well, I could not help it!" Sir Mark retorted, stung by this reproach from his beloved. "And as far as that goes, *you* seem to have lost your young charges, too. It is not easy to keep people always in sight in this curst maze!"

Regina was startled enough by this speech to forget her vexation and turn her attention upon Sir Mark instead, for never in her acquaintance with him had she seen him moved out of his perfect civility and good humour. As she stared at him, she saw a warm flush slowly mount into his face, and the next moment, to her amazement, he took an impetuous step forward and clasped her in his arms.

"Regina, my dearest love—listen to me! I *must* speak!" he said in an urgent voice. "If you think you can send me to play gooseberry for that pair of love-birds when all I want is to be with you—! You must know my feelings! I want you to be my wife—I've wished for nothing else since the first moment I laid eyes on you—"

"Oh, *dear!*" said Regina, struggling vainly against her admirer's manly embrace. "Sir Mark, *do* think what you are about! The custodian! He can see it all—!"

"Damn the custodian!" said Sir Mark, for, like all rather shy men, once he had begun he was so exhilarated by his own daring that he was a good deal more determined than a more experienced lover might have been.

And he implanted a masterful kiss upon her averted cheek, just as Bella suddenly came running into view at the end of the green alley. At sight of the tableau before her, she stopped short, transfixed.

"*Oh!*" she exclaimed. "How famous! You are going to marry Sir Mark! Oh, Reggie, how perfectly splendid for you!"

She ran forward towards the blushing pair, who had sprung apart on the instant, and flung her arms enthusiastically around Regina's neck. But before she could say any more an imperturbable voice behind her drawled, "So here you are, Bella!"— and Wrexam in turn strolled into view around a corner of the hedge walk. "Really, you are a troublesome chit," he said, "quite as bad as Maria—"

Bella, whirling to face him, did not allow him to finish his sentence.

"Oh, Alistair, isn't it famous?" she exclaimed. "Reggie is going to marry Sir Mark!"

"Going to marry Sir Mark?" repeated Wrexam, and Regina, already sufficiently discomposed by the turn of events, saw his eyes rest upon her with obviously amused incredulity. "Nonsense! She will do nothing of the sort," he continued, in the same maddeningly unruffled voice. "You are, as usual, jumping to conclusions, Bella."

Regina felt her back stiffen. "No, she is not! And I am! I mean, I *am* going to marry him!" she heard herself saying, to her own horrified amazement. But she would have done anything, *anything*, she felt at that moment, to erase that detestable look of amusement from Wrexam's face.

Which was perhaps as odd a reason for agreeing to marry someone as had ever been invented; but then proposals of marriage have a way of addling people's brains, both the makers and the receivers of them, to the extent that they are momentarily quite incapable of functioning in a rational manner.

At any rate, her words *did* have the effect of erasing the objectionable smile of amusement from Wrexam's face, for it was immediately replaced by a slight, quick frown. At the same instant Sir Mark, whom she had quite forgotten in her indignation with Wrexam, ejaculated, "Regina! My angel! You *will?*"—and, regardless of the presence of the others, as well as that of the presumably highly interested custodian in his Olympian stand above, he once more clasped her fervently in his arms.

This, Regina said to herself, *simply is not happening to me,* and she shut her eyes together firmly.

But when she opened them again, there was Sir Mark gazing at her with besotted fondness and still in possession of one of her hands, Bella looking as proud as if she had brought off the whole thing singlehanded, and Wrexam's face once more expressing nothing but a slightly mocking interest.

"You need say no more; I am quite convinced," he said. "Thurston, my felicitations. Mrs. Audwyn, may I be the first to wish you happy?"

Sir Mark, looking quite dazed with sudden bliss, said he was the most fortunate man in the world, while Regina, almost ready to sink in her consternation at what she had done, wondered miserably how one could explain to a worthy, well-meaning gentleman that one had agreed to marry him only because of a moment of madness which one could no more account for satisfactorily to oneself than one could to him. She walked as if in a dream through the succeeding minutes, while Giles and Maria were found and the news of her engagement to Sir Mark was communicated to them; and then they were all carried off to the Star and Garter by Sir Mark, where an excellent repast was bespoken for them, of which Regina, however, felt inclined to eat very little.

At the very earliest opportunity, she was telling herself, she would get Sir Mark alone and inform him, in the kindest way possible, that she could not marry him; and if he was justifiably angry with her and said the most cutting things that a gentleman could say to a lady under such circumstances it was, after all, she felt, no more than she deserved. She had behaved very badly—only of course it was all really Wrexam's fault, she told herself, for looking at her in that odiously smug way when Bella had made her announcement—and as a result of this conviction of his lordship's entire responsibility in the matter she showed such coolness to him during the remainder of the excursion that when they arrived back in Cavendish Square he took his leave without accepting her obviously very tepid invitation to come inside.

Not so Sir Mark, who was still in the first raptures of an accepted love, and would probably have come in whether he had been asked or not, following after his goddess with dazzled eyes. But in point of fact Regina *had* asked him, because she was planning on having her disagreeable explanation with him the moment she could rid herself of her young cousins; only, as it happened, her plans immediately went awry.

For they had no sooner stepped inside the front door than they were confronted by a very young and dishevelled gentleman none of them had ever seen before, who darted out of the morning-parlour, where he had evidently been lying in wait for them, and exclaimed, "Oh, Mrs. Audwyn! You *are* Mrs. Audwyn, aren't you? I'm most frightfully sorry and I did the best I could, only I got there too late, but the doctor says it's only a knock on the head—"

"What *are* you talking about?" Regina demanded, staring at him. "And who *are* you?"

The dishevelled young man, making an obvious effort to pull himself together, sketched a distracted bow.

"Oh!" he said. "Beg your pardon! Afraid I wasn't thinking! I'm Barny Crowcroft—I daresay you may have heard Colin speak of me?—and Colin asked me to go along with him to that house you have in Upper Wimpole Street. Search for d-diamonds, he said. All fun and gig. Only s-someone came in and hit him over the head when I wasn't by. Knocked him unconscious—but I got him home all right and tight, and the doctor says—"

But Regina was no longer attending to him; she had gathered up her skirts and fled up the stairs, intent upon seeing Colin at once for herself.

CHAPTER 10

She found her young cousin lying in bed with a bandage about his head and Miss Abthorpe seated beside him; but he bounced up into a sitting position at once upon her entrance into the room.

"Oh, I say, Reggie! Did Barny tell you what has happened?" he demanded eagerly. "There *is* someone after those diamonds! No doubt about it now! It's a deuced shame that he crept up behind me when he clouted me, because of course I didn't so much as get a glimpse of him myself—"

"Does Dr. Attwell say he ought to talk so much, Abby?" Regina enquired, advancing to the bed and looking anxiously into Colin's face, which was certainly rather pale but appeared quite as cheerful as ever.

"No," said Miss Abthorpe composedly. "But it is quite useless to expect him to be quiet until he has told his tale to you. Sit down, my dear; it is really not so bad as it seems, you know. I do not know what that poor young man downstairs has been telling you—"

"Very little, I am afraid, except that Colin was struck on the head by someone in Upper Wimpole Street—"

"It was the same fellow Wrexam saw there yesterday—there can be no doubt of *that!*" Colin interrupted. "Of course *I* didn't see him, because he came up on me from behind, but Barny did, and his description of him fits Wrexam's exactly. A young man, with black hair—and what's more, Barny is almost certain that he cried out something in French as he grappled with him. Of course it might *not* have been French, because Barny's not much of a dab at languages, but at any rate it seems he must be some sort of foreigner—"

Regina, putting an end at this point to her young cousin's pell-mell speech, said severely that if he did not stop exciting himself and settle down to give her a calm description of exactly what had happened she would go away and he would not be able to tell her anything at all.

"Oh, very well!" said Colin indulgently. "Not that there's really much to tell, you know. You remember I went to Upper Wimpole Street to have another look round this afternoon, and I thought I'd just take Barny with me, because we might make a better job of it between the two of us. Well, we'd been searching for more than an hour without finding anything, and I was in the drawing room, looking over that rum fireplace—the one with the carved figures of Paris and Venus—to see if the diamonds could have been hidden there somehow, while Barny was still upstairs in one of the bedrooms. After a while I heard someone come into the room behind me, but of course I thought it was Barny, so I didn't trouble to look round. I began to say something to him, and the next thing I knew I was hit over the head from behind. Barny told me afterwards that when he came in he found the fellow bending over me with a good stout cudgel still in his hand, and of course Barny's a well-plucked 'un so he went for him, and they had a bit of a tussle and then the fellow broke away and ran out of the house. Barny didn't go after him because he had me to think of—well, he didn't know how badly off I was, you see—and by the time he'd brought me around it was too late. But he says he thinks he might know the fellow if he saw him again, and his description of him tallies exactly with Wrexam's description of the man *he* saw in the house yesterday. So don't you see, Reggie, it must be someone who is after the diamonds! *I* think we ought to keep a watch on the house—"

"And *I* think," said Regina firmly, "that we shall do nothing of the sort! I am *not* going to have you murdered because of a necklace that belongs to neither of us! If the Comte wishes to have the house watched I shall have no objection if he arranges to do so, and I shall most certainly tell him what occurred there today—but *you* are to have no more to do with those diamonds, Colin! Good heavens, don't you see that you might have been killed?"

"Gammon! One doesn't die of a clout over the head," Colin said scornfully. "Besides, whoever he is, he can have no wish to kill me, or anyone else, for how would that serve him? All he wants is the necklace."

"And all *I* want," Regina said, "is to see an end to this absurd business! I know nothing about those diamonds, and I certainly knew nothing of that house in Upper Wimpole Street until the Comte told me of it, and now I wish to know nothing more! I shall give him the key and he may do whatever he likes with it, but *we* shall do nothing further in the matter."

In vain did Colin protest that this was the most exciting thing that had happened to him since he had come to London; in vain did he point out how poor-spirited it would be of them to allow the intruder, whoever he was, to carry off the diamonds without making the least push to stop him. Regina was adamant. It was the Comte's affair, not theirs, she said; she would see him on the following day and turn over the key to him, and what happened after that would be entirely in his hands.

Meanwhile, the thought of her engagement to Sir Mark had been driven completely out of her head, but when she had left Colin's room, after persuading him with some difficulty to swallow the draught that Dr. Attwell had left for him, the remembrance of it recurred to her with disagreeable force, and she was a good deal disappointed, when she went downstairs once more, to learn that Sir Mark had been obliged to depart, having been summoned by an urgent message from one of his servants. His mother, whom he had left at his house in Kent, was ill, it appeared, and he had gone off to her at once, leaving a message for Regina regretting his inability to escort her to the ball Lady Jersey was giving at Osterley that evening.

Regina, who had been counting upon having her explanation with him without delay, before the news of her acceptance of his suit could spread to anyone else beyond the few persons who now knew of it, felt that nothing more vexatious could have occurred. Of course Sir Mark would tell his mother and any other members of his family whom he chanced to meet in Kent about his offer to her and its successful outcome, and there was no knowing how far the story might go before she could have the opportunity to inform him that she really could not be his wife, after all.

But there was nothing that could be done now, since Sir Mark had gone, except to caution Bella to say nothing of the matter to anyone at Osterley that evening.

"But why mayn't I?" Bella enquired, opening her eyes very wide. "*I* shall certainly tell everyone as soon as Alistair and I are really engaged."

"*If* you ever become engaged to Lord Wrexam, you may do as you like," Regina said. "But in this case, I—I find that I have made a mistake, and I shall tell Sir Mark so as soon as the opportunity offers. You can see, then, how embarrassing it will be for both of us if you spread the tale about—"

"Then you *aren't* going to marry him?" Bella interrupted incredulously. "But whatever made you tell him you would, then? If *I* were to get engaged to someone, and then decide to get *un*engaged the next moment, you would say I was a silly child, and too young to know my own mind. But you aren't a child, and have been married before—"

"Having been married before doesn't prevent one from behaving quite as foolishly as if one were seventeen, when it comes to *Men*," Regina said darkly. "I have acted very stupidly, but don't, pray, make the matter worse by telling anyone else of it!"

"Well," said Bella practically, "I won't, then, but it seems to me that you are very foolish not to have Sir Mark. He is excessively good-humoured, and does everything you wish him to without making the least fuss about it, which must be very agreeable in a husband. Do you think I shall ever be able to bring Alistair to that pass?"

"If you are ever able," Regina said feelingly, "to bring Lord Wrexam to consider anyone or anything but his own convenience, you will have performed the greatest miracle in nature!"

But in this she was doing his lordship an injustice, for the first thing he enquired of her, when he came upon her at Osterley that evening, was if he could be of any further service to her in the matter of the Chelles diamonds.

"No!" said Regina, and then immediately temporised and said, "Well, perhaps," for she was sadly in need, she felt, of someone to whom to confide the latest of the misadventures to which those unfortunate diamonds had led. Besides, she thought, Wrexam, who had seen both Lescot and the housebreaker, might be able to resolve the disagreeable doubt the Comte had implanted in her mind as to whether the two might be one and the same person.

So without demur she allowed him to lead her from the ballroom, where the musicians had just begun to play a waltz and couples were circling about the polished floor in a kaleidoscope of fashionable pale colours, into the beautiful, deserted library, where the rows of heavy volumes, their calf bindings polished to a dull gold, stood serenely in their serried ranks, framed by the white columns and classical entablatures of the Vitruvian bookcases.

"I feel sure," Wrexam remarked, "that, despite the fact that we are quite alone, even Thurston would consider us adequately chaperoned here, surrounded as we are by so much of the world's wit and wisdom. It is my contention that no one has ever been seduced in a proper library. The atmosphere simply is not conducive. By the bye," he continued, "where *is* Thurston this evening? I trust he has not deserted you so soon?"

"He is gone to Kent," said Regina. "His mother is ill," and why she did not immediately add that she had decided not to be engaged to him, after all, only the twin demons of stubbornness and pride that had her in their grip at the moment knew. It was most definitely her duty so to inform him, she was aware, for if she did not he might very well go about all evening telling people about the projected match; but she simply could not bring herself to see his lordship looking the words, "I told you so," at her, even if he did not actually say them.

So she contented herself with the brief explanation she had already uttered, and Wrexam, after regarding her rather quizzically for a moment, said, "Indeed? It is just as well, I daresay.

I should find it difficult to play the rejected suitor this evening—
you haven't forgotten, I hope, that I am presumed to be nursing
a hopeless passion for you?—since in point of fact I am feeling
rather particularly cheerful"—which speech, implying as it did
his lordship's entire satisfaction with a state of affairs promi-
nently featuring her engagement to Sir Mark, struck her as being,
for some reason which she would have found it difficult to explain, a rather disagreeable and even unfeeling one. "I hope," his
lordship continued, apparently quite unconscious of the unfavourable feelings his words had occasioned, "that you and the
Dowager Lady Thurston will contrive to deal tolerably well with
each other. Thurston, I understand, is a model of all the filial
virtues and she appears to be accustomed to receiving the most
assiduous attentions from him. But you are acquainted with her
yourself, I expect?"

"No, I am not," said Regina rather shortly.

"Well, she is said to be something of a Tartar—but then one
can't have everything exactly as one likes it in life—can one?"
Wrexam remarked. "After all, Thurston is a well-set-up fellow,
with an excellent temper, and of course you are aware that he is
swimming in lard—"

"I am *not* interested in Sir Mark's fortune, Lord Wrexam!"
Regina said, somewhat nettled by what she took to be an insinu-
ation against the purity of her motives in accepting Sir Mark's
proposal.

"Of course you are not. No lady ever is," Wrexam said soothingly. "Still it is comforting, when the marriage vows have
been spoken, to be able to reflect that if one has taken a dead
bore for a husband, he is at least a very rich dead bore."

"Sir Mark is *not* a dead bore! He is—he is an exceedingly sensible man, with an excellent understanding!"

"You are quite right: he is," Wrexam cordially agreed. "In
point of fact, half the dead bores of my acquaintance are sensible men with excellent understandings; those qualifications are
essential, it seems, for boring one's friends. Fools and eccentrics
are usually far more amusing."

"Which is no doubt why you, my lord, are universally admitted to be such entertaining company!" said Regina quite unforgivably.

But his lordship only said, "No—am I? I rather doubt it; I don't appear to succeed in amusing *you*, at any rate. You usually look at me with what I should call a somewhat smouldering expression in those remarkably speaking eyes of yours, rather, I should say if pressed to define it, as if you would like to hit me."

"Well, I should!" said Regina feelingly. "Very frequently! But I didn't come here to discuss such matters with you, Lord Wrexam. What I wish you to tell me is if you believe there is any possibility that the housebreaker you surprised in Upper Wimpole Street yesterday and Gervais Lescot are one and the same man."

Wrexam put up his brows. "Lescot?" he said. "What has caused you to take that notion into your head?"

Regina forthwith launched into the tale of Colin's misadventures, of the conversation she had had that morning with the Comte de Chelles, and of the Comte's certainty that he had told no one but his nephew of the suspected presence of the diamonds in the house in Upper Wimpole Street.

"And Mr. Lescot certainly heard Colin discussing his plans this morning for searching the house again today," she said; "in fact, Colin invited him to go with him, but he refused. Which," she said, wrinkling her brows, "is exactly what he would have done—wouldn't he?—if he had made his own plans to lie in wait at the house and watch to see if Colin really did succeed in finding the diamonds, and then make off with them in such a way that Colin would never see who had taken them. The thing that puzzles me about the matter is that Colin says he found nothing at all in the house, so why should the housebreaker, or Lescot, or whoever it was, have struck him down from behind and then, apparently, have been bending over him to search him when Mr. Crowcroft came into the room?"

Wrexam did not reply. He was looking, she saw, unwontedly thoughtful, which for some reason made her feel suddenly anxious.

"Oh!" she said involuntarily. "You *do* think Lescot is the housebreaker! You think *he* struck Colin—"

"Not at all," Wrexam said dampingly. "I have no fixed opinion on the matter as yet. The glimpse I had of the man was not sufficient to allow me to identify him as Lescot or anyone else, and the evidence you yourself are bringing against him is extremely circumstantial, to say the least. Young Mr. Crowcroft, now, might be helpful to you, since he must have a fairly good notion of the man's appearance."

Regina looked doubtful. "Yes, I daresay he has," she said. "But on the other hand he has never met Mr. Lescot, and I must say he seems a rather excitable young man, and *not* what I should call a reliable witness."

"All the same," said Wrexam, "it might be as well to put the matter to the test. Can you arrange in some plausible way to have the two meet in Cavendish Square? You have invited Lescot, I daresay, to Bella's ball next week? Send an invitation to young Crowcroft as well."

"Yes, I might do that," Regina agreed. "But, good God, if it turns out that he *does* identify Lescot as the man who attacked Colin, what am I to do? I can't very well send for a constable and have him taken up!"

"We shall cross that bridge when we come to it," Wrexam said, dismissing the subject. "Meanwhile, though, there is something else that I wish you to do. Will you send a message to the Comte de Chelles tomorrow morning that you have something of importance to communicate to him and would like him to call upon you in Cavendish Square at eleven? Precisely at eleven—do you understand?"

Regina stared at him. "No, I don't understand in the least!" she said. "Why at eleven? And what am I to tell him when he comes?"

"At eleven because I have told you to do so," Wrexam said, with an air of considering that quite enough to say on the subject. "And you know very well what you can tell him when he comes—about Colin's misadventures in Upper Wimpole Street."

"Well, I had already intended to do *that*," Regina agreed, but still nettled over being kept in the dark as to his lordship's plans. "As a matter of fact, I have made up my mind to give him the key to the wretched place—"

"Give him the key?" Wrexam interrupted her without ceremony. "No, you will certainly not do that!"

"Not—!" Regina looked at him indignantly. "Lord Wrexam," she said distinctly, after a moment, "it is *not* your prerogative to tell me what I will or will not do! If I wish to give the key of that house to the Comte de Chelles, I shall do so and there is an end to the matter!"

Wrexam shrugged. "Very well," he said. "If you wish to behave like a nodcock, that is *your* prerogative, Mrs. Audwyn. I daresay it will make no difference in the end, at any rate. The house is certainly not proof against anyone who wishes to enter it, as has already been demonstrated more than once. And I expect it would be quite useless to ask you to have it made so."

"Quite useless," said Regina with dignity. "I have told you that it is my intention to hand the key over to the Comte and have nothing more to do with the whole abominable business. I daresay you will be telling me next that you suspect the Comte of trying to steal his own diamonds!" she added as a parting shot, and, getting up, she walked out of the room, fuming at herself for having put herself in the position of once more inviting Wrexam to interfere in her affairs.

Of course she would send no message to the Comte on the following day, she told herself as she sought out Bella, whom she found, with the weathercock perversity of the very young, dancing with Lescot. The two young people appeared to be quarrelling with each other, as usual, and Regina, remembering the high hopes she had had of seeing her cousin tumble into love with one of the extremely eligible *partis* to whom she had introduced her, thought in despair that it was just like a Stacpoole to ignore the bouquets and invitations lavished upon her by unexceptionable young noblemen and divide her time instead between Wrexam and a young man whom she professed to dislike cordially, and who, for all they knew, might be little better than a common adventurer.

She managed to manoeuvre Bella into standing up for the quadrille with young Lord Holt, who had half a dozen rivals for the honour, any of whom, Regina thought exasperatedly, would have been embraced as a son-in-law by Lord Arun with the greatest enthusiasm; but the evening, as far as she personally was concerned, was already a dismal failure. There was her explanation with Sir Mark looming before her, Colin lying in Cavendish Square with a broken head, Bella stubbornly refusing to behave as one hoped she would, and Wrexam issuing mysterious orders that must have something to do with those troublesome diamonds. What more, she thought, could occur to set her on end?

It was a question that was very soon to be answered.

CHAPTER
11

It was, in fact, answered the moment she and Bella arrived back in Cavendish Square that evening. The front door was opened to them, as usual, by Hughes, but before they had well crossed the threshold the hall was invaded by a rush of young Stacpooles, with Nannie bringing up the rear in a futile attempt to stem the tide of their progress.

"Reggie! Reggie! We have had a *housebreaker!*" Maria shrieked, exhibiting her stout form in a flannel dressing gown, with her fair hair in its stiff pigtails almost standing on end with excitement, while Giles, similarly attired in night-gear, jigged up and down in sympathetic enthusiasm. "He came into Giles's bed-chamber, and Nannie heard him and came and hit him over the head with her umbrella, and he ran away! And we have had a constable—"

"Now, Lady Maria, you are to come upstairs to bed this very minute!" Nannie scolded, arriving on the scene and attempting to seize her young charge's hand.

But Maria, flown with the heady aura of crime and being out of her bed in the middle of the night, was for once impervious to the voice of authority and flung her arms about Regina's waist instead, clinging to her like a drowning mariner to a rock.

"I won't!" she proclaimed recalcitrantly. "Not until I've told Reggie and Bella about the housebreaker! I *saw* him, Reggie! He was enormously tall, and wore a black mask over his face, and had a pistol—"

"Now, Lady Maria!" said Nannie again severely. "That will be quite enough. We all know what happens to young ladies who tell stories." She said to Regina over Maria's head, with an unwonted air of distraction, "Really, Miss Regina, I'm that upset with all this that I don't know if I'm on my head or on my heels! Here I've only just got Master Colin back to his bed, that *would* insist on getting up to see what all the commotion was about, and Miss Trimingham safe in hers, after such a fit of the hysterics as you wouldn't believe, when what must these two do but slip out of the nursery the minute my back was turned—"

"But, good God, is it true, then?" Regina asked. "The house has really been broken into—?"

"Not *broken into,* so to speak, ma'am, being as the kitchen window was left open by the hall-boy, who should have been asleep in *his* bed but wasn't," said Nannie grimly, "being gone out without leave and *what* he may have been doing never ask me, for they're never too young for devilment, in *my* experience."

But at that moment, much to Regina's relief, Miss Abthorpe, fully dressed in a very proper grey gown with a lace fichu at the neck, came in and proceeded to take charge of the situation.

"Maria—Giles—you are to go upstairs with Nannie at once," she said in the calm voice of one who has been dealing with the young for so many years that she is quite capable of looking straight into their heads like a kindly but perfectly adamant sorceress. "There will be no more housebreakers tonight, and if you do not go to bed straight away you will not be able to tell your cousin about what has happened in the morning."

Maria, looking mutinous, said she wanted to tell her now, and how did Abby know the housebreaker would not come back?

"Because," said Miss Abthorpe, "he would not be so foolish, besides having had his pride hurt by having been hit over the head with an umbrella. Housebreakers are very sensitive to such slights, you know."

"Have *you* ever seen a housebreaker, Abby?" Giles demanded suspiciously.

"Oh dear, yes. Upon several occasions. There was a particularly disagreeable one at Hawksworth Towers when I was instructing the Marchioness's three daughters, who knocked the second footman down the third-storey pair of stairs while he was carrying a decanter of port up to his lordship. It quite spoiled the carpet. I shall tell you all about it in the morning."

And she detached Maria firmly from her hold on Regina and handed her over to Nannie, who sailed off with her and Giles up the stairs.

Miss Abthorpe turned to Regina. "And now, my dear," she said, "let us go into the morning-parlour and I shall tell you exactly what occurred—or as nearly, at any rate, as I have been able to make it out from what Nannie and the children have had to say, for of course I knew nothing of it until it was over. Really most unfortunate, for Nannie is not at all accustomed to dealing with such matters and I fear rather lost her head—"

"Did she *really* hit him over the head with her umbrella, Abby?" Bella demanded, following her and Regina into the morning-parlour and perching upon the arm of the chair in which her cousin seated herself.

"Not having any other weapon at hand when she heard noises coming from Giles's bedchamber, I regret to say, yes," replied Miss Abthorpe, who had also composedly sat down, crossed her ankles neatly, and folded her hands together in her lap. "She found the intruder turning out the box in which Giles's toys are customarily stored and attacked him before he was aware of her presence."

"I—*say!*" said Bella enthusiastically. "Good for Nannie!"

"It had the effect, at any rate," said Miss Abthorpe, looking at her disapprovingly, "of preventing any further depredations, for the intruder then fled down the stairs and left the house by the same window by which he appears to have entered it. As far as can be ascertained, no damage was done except to the large Chinese vase that lives on the malachite table in the first-storey hall, which he knocked to the floor in his flight but fortunately did not break except for one of the handles. Nothing appears to be missing from Giles's bedchamber."

"But—but this is all perfectly preposterous, Abby!" Regina protested, her eyes now almost as wide as Bella's. "Why on earth should a housebreaker—any housebreaker—go to a small boy's room in search of valuables? Of all the unlikely places—!"

"I quite agree with you, my dear," said Miss Abthorpe. "But I fancy, you see, that he was not an ordinary housebreaker."

"You mean he was *Colin's* housebreaker—that he was looking for the diamonds?" said Regina incredulously. "But, Abby, why should he have thought they were *here?*—and in Giles's bedchamber, of all places? Surely he must realise that if Colin *had* found the diamonds, they would not have been left in a box of toys!"

"Yes, my dear; I know all that. Still, by Nannie's description, he *was* a young, active man, with black hair—"

"That is all very well," said Regina firmly, "but I daresay there must be hundreds of housebreakers in London, and most of them are young and active, and probably half of them, at least, are dark. I simply refuse to believe it is not a mere coincidence. Unless," she went on, as a sudden horrid thought occurred to her, "he is a madman who has found out somehow about the diamonds and has no discretion at all in looking for them. But if that is so—"

"I am quite certain it is *not* so, my dear Regina," Miss Abthorpe said with equal firmness. "The person who entered the house tonight came here, I am sure, with a very definite purpose in mind, for he obviously made his way straight to the nursery floor without the least attempt at ransacking any of the other rooms. What reason he can have had for believing there was anything of value there I cannot say, but we may be assured, I believe, that he did indeed have a reason."

Bella, who appeared to have been mulling over in her mind which of several highly coloured interpretations, based upon the complexities of lending-library fiction, might best be placed upon the mysterious incident, here gave it as her opinion that the intruder had been a kidnaper, bent upon holding Giles to ransom, and that his purpose in rummaging in Giles's toy-box had been to find some bauble that would serve to beguile and console his victim during the abduction.

"Really, my dear!" said Miss Abthorpe mildly. "I cannot think where you come by such odd notions! Pray do not be putting such ideas into the children's heads. You will not wish to frighten them, I am sure!"

Bella said there was no fear of that, for she was sure Giles would like above all things to be kidnaped—which came so near the truth that Regina could not help laughing and Miss Abthorpe sensibly said that was quite enough and they might all go to bed now and talk about what was to be done in the morning.

"I have, of course," she said, "already informed the Authorities, who have assured me that everything possible will be done to prevent a recurrence of this unfortunate incident, and, what is perhaps more to the point, I have spoken to Hughes about seeing to it that the house is properly locked up at night. If, in spite of these precautions, the intruder should manage to return," she added tranquilly, "I daresay he will do no one any harm unless interfered with, as he obviously wishes only to find the diamonds."

This was scant comfort to Regina, who well knew that not only Colin, but also Giles and Maria, would like nothing better than to interfere with the housebreaker, should he chance to cross their paths, and she was plagued, in addition, by that nagging doubt as to whether the housebreaker might in reality be Lescot. Certainly he had been at Osterley that evening, but equally certainly he had taken his departure early, for she herself had seen him making his adieux to Lady Jersey at an hour shortly past midnight. He would thus have had ample time to drive back to town and be in Cavendish Square at two, which was the hour when Nannie had surprised the housebreaker in Giles's bedchamber.

The upshot of these reflections was—somewhat illogically, for she could not see what connexion it might have with solving the mystery of the housebreaker—a determination to do as Wrexam had asked, and send a message to the Comte de Chelles requesting him to come to Cavendish Square at eleven in the morning. If she could not fathom the reason for this stratagem of Wrexam's, at least it appeared that he was working on some plan, and, as she had none of her own at present, she had nothing to lose by following his.

She accordingly sent a footman with her message in the morning to Fenton's Hotel, where the Comte was staying, and soon received in return a polite assurance that the Comte would be happy to comply with her request and would wait upon her at eleven. She did not know whether to expect that Wrexam, too, would appear upon her doorstep at that hour, but she had little opportunity to ponder the matter, for Colin, much recovered from his encounter the day before with the Upper Wimpole Street intruder, came downstairs looking for her so that he might discuss with her his own theories of the mystery, which were quite as fanciful as Bella's, and only by the combined authority of Nannie and Miss Abthorpe was he at last bullied back into his bed again.

Then there was the nursery party to be coped with, still full of the previous night's excitement, and the caterer and the florist to be interviewed over the preparations for Bella's ball on the morrow; and the result was that when the Comte arrived at eleven she was thinking more of lobster patties and tubs of lilies than of diamonds, and was brought up rather short by the Comte's demand to see them at once.

"See the diamonds?" she repeated, looking at him blankly and wishing, as she did every time she met him, that his eyes didn't bore though one so. "But—I can't—"

"You have found them—*n'est-ce pas?*" the Comte insisted. "That is why you have send for me?"

"Oh, no—no!" Regina disclaimed hurriedly. "I have *not* send—*sent* for you for *that* reason!"

"Then why—?"

The Comte looked at her so suspiciously that Regina made haste to launch into her tale of the mysterious intruder who had attacked Colin in the house in Upper Wimpole Street, and of their nocturnal visitor of the previous night. The Comte appeared to grow more and more agitated during this recital, and at its conclusion considerably startled her by enquiring abruptly if she would allow him to make a search of the premises himself so that he might satisfy himself that the diamonds were indeed not there.

"A search of the premises?" Regina repeated. "Do you mean the house in Upper Wimpole Street?"

"No! This house!" said the Comte, with such emphasis that Regina suddenly found herself wishing that Wrexam *would* appear upon her doorstep and take a hand in the matter himself. "Also to question your young cousin—Milord St. Cyres, is it?—as to what he has removed from the *other* house. He has—like all young gentlemen, *hein?*—the pleasure to make the joke. *Hein?*" he repeated, with so much sinister emphasis upon the syllable that Regina started.

"No, I don't think so—and as a matter of fact I haven't the least notion what you are talking of!" she said, almost too surprised to be indignant. "Do you mean that you think Colin has found the diamonds and has said nothing to anyone of it? But that is absurd!"

"Ah! It may be absurd, Madame, but yet it may also be true!" said the Comte, rising to come across the room and wag his finger menacingly under her nose. "It is absurd—is it not?—that I, a nobleman of France, am obliged to sue to you for the return of these diamonds, the sole pittance remaining from a great fortune that has been robbed from me by Fate! Nevertheless, it is true! So you will please to show me this young man, Madame; you will please to show me his effects and those of his young brother and sister—"

What might have occurred next had they been left to themselves was debatable, for obviously the Comte had no intention of abandoning his preposterous determination to interview Colin and search his bedchamber; but at that moment, to Regina's intense relief, Hughes appeared in the doorway to announce, "Lord Wrexam!"

"Oh!" said Regina. "Show him in at once, Hughes, please!" —whereupon the Comte impressed her by audibly grinding his teeth in a manner that she had previously considered reserved only to villains in melodramas.

"This will not do, Madame!" he began in a furious voice; but just then Wrexam, extremely well turned out, as usual, in a coat of exquisite fit, gleaming Hessians, and the palest of biscuit pantaloons, strolled into the room.

A rather odd little scene—at least to Regina's way of thinking— then took place. She herself was obliged to begin it by making the two men known to each other, an introduction which was received by Wrexam with an appearance of some interest, and by the Comte with the hasty and frustrated air of a man who has been interrupted in the pursuance of important business and has no intention of allowing himself to be long diverted from his purpose.

Wrexam, however, who had seated himself in an armchair across from the Comte's, at once accomplished the difficult feat of deflecting him completely from his present preoccupation by uttering in a negligent voice a very simple and apparently quite harmless pair of sentences.

"I have just," he remarked, "had the pleasure of a conversation with a very old friend of yours, Comte. You will remember Madame du Grandjean, I am sure?"

The effect upon the Comte of this innocent query was startling. His long face, which had at best a rather cadaverous colour, grew chalk-white, and a hunted look appeared in his deep-set eyes. After a moment he gabbled, "Ah! Madame du Grandjean! *Mais certainement! Certainement!* She is well, I hope! It has been a great many years—"

"So she has told me," said Wrexam, giving no sign that he observed anything peculiar in the Comte's reaction to his words and speaking instead with the cheerful air of a man uttering social commonplaces for the entertainment of his acquaintances. "But she remembers *you* perfectly, she tells me, Comte. A remarkable woman! She must be close upon eighty, but a mind as clear as a bell. She is looking forward to renewing her acquaintance with you during your stay in London, she says."

"*Mais certainement! Certainement!*" said the Comte once more, but with such a terrified air of not comprehending in the least what he was saying that Regina stared at him in astonishment. He then threw himself back in his chair, grinned at Wrexam as if defying the Fates, and said with obvious bravado, "Madame du Grandjean was a frequent visitor at the Château de Chelles. Yes, yes! I have often had the pleasure of seeing her there! But my health—my health! It is extremely poor, you understand. It prevents me from going a great deal into society at present!"

"Unfortunate!" murmured Wrexam. "But in the case of so old a friend—"

"Yes, yes! I shall be delighted to see Madame du Grandjean. *Certainement! Certainement!*" the Comte again declared hastily. He rose suddenly. "But now I must take my leave. You understand—my health—it is my health. Madame"—he bowed meaningly over Regina's hand—"I shall do myself the honour soon of waiting upon you again."

And before Regina could recover from her surprise at this abrupt reversal of what had been his obvious determination to remain in the house until she had acceded to his demand to see Colin and his room, he had hastily bowed himself out.

Regina looked blankly at Wrexam. "And what," she enquired, "is the meaning of all that? You are looking extraordinarily smug!"

"Am I? Yes, I daresay I am," Wrexam agreed. "It is always highly satisfying to have one's theories confirmed by fact. Was he causing you trouble?" he added with an interested air.

"Well, in point of fact, he was!" said Regina. "He seems to have taken the mad notion into his head that Colin actually found the diamonds in Upper Wimpole Street yesterday and now has them hidden somewhere in his bedchamber! But what theory are you talking of? And why confirmed by fact? Do you mean that *you* know where the diamonds are?"

"Not in the least," said Wrexam. "As a matter of fact, I am not even sure that there are any diamonds. But I am now quite certain of one thing, and that is that, whether there are diamonds or not, there is assuredly no Comte de Chelles."

"No Comte de Chelles?" Regina stared at him. "But, my dear man, you have just met him!"

"I have just met," Wrexam corrected her, "a person who calls himself the Comte de Chelles. You *do* see that there may be a slight difference?"

He looked at Regina, who looked back at him with a thunderstruck air.

"A slight difference!" she repeated after a moment, in a dazed voice. "Then you mean—he is *not* the Comte de Chelles?"

"Not," said Wrexam scrupulously, "unless he has managed to

shrink several inches, grow a pair of extraordinarily black eyebrows, and remodel his nose from Roman to snub during the past twenty years. It has been approximately that long since Madame du Grandjean has seen the Comte, but, though a very old lady, she is in remarkably good possession of all her faculties, and she assures me that the man she saw entering this house a short time ago, as she sat with me in her carriage just outside your door, bore not the slightest resemblance to the man she had known for many years in France as the Comte de Chelles."

Regina was almost too stunned to say anything, but feeling that something was required of her said if he wasn't the Comte de Chelles then who was he, and why in the world had he said he was?

"To get his hands on the diamonds, obviously," Wrexam said. "*He* certainly believes in them, though I am not sure that I do. As to who he actually is—Madame du Grandjean can't be certain of that, but she has an idea he may be the Comte's agent, a man named Jobin, whom she recalls having seen occasionally on her visits to the Château de Chelles. Those eyebrows rather stick in one's memory, you see. And *that* theory squares rather nicely, too, with the story Lescot gave you of the Comte's having been accompanied on his flight to America by a pair of retainers, one of whom was that very agent. Lescot told you he died during the voyage and was buried at sea—but let us suppose, for the sake of argument, that it was the Comte and not the agent who actually died, and that the agent, with the connivance of his fellow-servant, concocted a plan to assume his master's identity in a strange country none of them had ever visited before. He would be, you see, in possession of all the Comte's papers, which would really make it child's play for him to carry the imposture off, and even if he did not then have the plan for recovering the diamonds already in his mind—he had not yet heard at the time, it appears, of your husband's death—it must have seemed to him that being the Comte de Chelles might be considerably more advantageous to him, even in America, than being plain Monsieur Jobin."

Regina, who had been following this exposition with a sinking heart, said, "And Lescot? Do you think he is in it, too? That he is the other servant, for example?"

"As to that, I haven't the least notion as yet," Wrexam said. "He is far too young for Madame du Grandjean to have known him, and New Orleans is several thousand miles away, so that it is rather difficult to find someone at once who can vouch for his being the man he claims to be. We shall try your young friend Crowcroft tomorrow, at any rate, on the matter of whether he was the housebreaker in Upper Wimpole Street."

This made Regina recall that she had not yet told Wrexam about their own housebreaker of the previous night, and she related the whole tale to him, adding that Nannie, of course, had actually seen the intruder, but that, as on this occasion he had worn a mask, she was unable to identify him as anyone she had ever seen before.

"Young, active, black-haired—that is all we seem to come back to, in every case," she said unhappily, "and that description certainly fits Mr. Lescot. But he does seem a very nice young man, not in the least like the Comte—I mean M. Jobin."

Wrexam said rather unsympathetically that a great many thoroughgoing scoundrels were able to give the appearance of being very nice young men, which was, for some of them, their stock in trade, but that he was willing to give young Lescot the benefit of the doubt until he was able to find out more about him.

"Not, though, to the extent of handing over the diamonds to him if they *do* turn up," he said. "If he actually is the real Comte's nephew and heir, of course, he will have the right to lay claim to them. By the way, you *are* quite sure, I suppose, that Colin didn't come home with them yesterday? Our friend Jobin has seemed to have remarkably accurate information in the matter up to this time—in the present case, no doubt, at the expense of a small bribe to your hall-boy. I should get rid of that enterprising young man, if I were you."

Regina said she agreed with him perfectly on that point, but that she was quite sure Colin would not have concealed the fact that he had found the diamonds from her if he actually had. She then asked practically what they were to do about the matter of the false Comte.

"I daresay he has really not done anything to be taken up for, except saying that he is the Comte de Chelles when he isn't," she

said, "and I expect he hasn't said *that* to anyone but us, because
Mr. Lescot tells me that he doesn't go about in society at all. And
it would be rather horrid to have a scandal about it, wouldn't it?
—because after all the real Comte *was* Etienne's uncle, and, besides, I don't think Uncle Ned would like me to have a scandal
now, just when Bella is making her come-out."

"Unless it is one he makes himself," Wrexam said disre-
spectfully, but added, "Very well; we shan't have a scandal,
then, both for Bella's sake and for yours. We shall think instead
of a way to get rid of the Comte quietly, and with the utmost respectability."

"Well, I *don't* think he will go away without the diamonds,"
Regina said doubtfully. "Especially since he doesn't know that
Madame du Grandjean has already seen him and told you he
isn't really a proper Comte."

Upon which Wrexam said, with what she considered an exas-
perating lack of appreciation of the seriousness of the matter,
that if he wouldn't go away without them he must go away with
them, and then compounded his flippancy by changing the subject and asking if she had had any word as yet from Sir Mark.

"Of course not!" she said loftily. "Nor, may I say, do I expect
any! After all, he has not been four-and-twenty hours away from
me!"

Wrexam shook his head, looking, she thought, odiously superior and sympathetic. "My dear girl," he pointed out, "a really
ardent lover would have had a messenger pelting back to you
from the first posting-house where he changed horses, bearing a
poem to your charms composed on the way!"

"And what," retorted Regina with considerable spirit, "do *you*
know of ardent love, Lord Wrexam?"

"More than you think, my child. More than you think," replied
Wrexam most unexpectedly, and there was a glint in his dark
eyes as he said it that made Regina think with a sudden odd
pang that Bella really was a very lucky girl, and at the same
time, for no apparent reason, wish poor prosy Sir Mark at the
devil.

CHAPTER 12

Sir Mark, however, was not at the devil, but with his mother in Kent—or at least so Regina thought until the following morning, when Hughes bore a card in to her in the morning-parlour, where she had been riding the whirlwind and directing the storm in the matter of preparations for Bella's ball that evening.

"Lady Thurston!" she said when she had looked at it. She raised her eyes to Hughes with an expression of astonishment in them. "But how can it be—? She is ill in Kent!"

"Apparently," suggested Hughes, with the magisterial calm that had carried him through thirty years of crises at Bellacourt House, "she has recovered, ma'am. If, of course, the lady I have shown into the library—the other rooms being in some disarray owing to the preparations for this evening's festivities—really *is* Lady Thurston—"

"But of course she is Lady Thurston!" said Regina, her mind boggling at the notion of a bogus Dowager added to a bogus Comte. "I have never met her, but—of course it must be, no matter how strange it seems!" She rose. "In the library, you said? I had best go to her at once."

And she hurried off, her heart sinking at the thought of the interview before her.

How, she asked herself, was she to break the news to this unknown female, who had doubtless hurried up to town to welcome her into the family the moment her son had informed her of his engagement, that she really had not the least intention of marrying him? It seemed quite impossible to do so, yet the alternative—accepting Lady Thurston's felicitations and allowing her to believe that she would soon be walking down the aisle of St. George's, Hanover Square, to meet Sir Mark at the altar—was equally unthinkable.

If only, she thought, this visit had not come upon her so suddenly, so that she might have had time to arrange her thoughts a little! But obviously there was no time, and it was accordingly a rather *distrait* Regina who entered the library and advanced towards the large lady who sat facing the door in a militantly upright position, rather overpowering her surroundings in a beehive bonnet of moss-straw trimmed with a forest of curled plumes.

"Good morning, Lady Thurston," she said, in what she hoped was a composed and civil tone. "I am sorry you have found us in such a state of turmoil, but you see my young cousin is making her come-out this Season and we are giving a ball in her honour tonight—"

She broke off; she had suddenly become aware that Lady Thurston's countenance, far from expressing the complaisance of a lady who had come to extend a maternal welcome to her son's chosen bride, was set in lines that were not only rigid, but positively inimical. Her rather small mouth which primmed up in her plump face, and her grey eyes—which, in their own way, were quite as uncomfortably penetrating as M. Jobin's—took in, through the face-à-main she had raised to them, every detail of Regina's appearance as if she were itemising them and ticking down an unfavourable comment after each.

"Mrs. Audwyn?" she responded to Regina's greeting, in a voice that emphasised the disapproval apparent in her demeanour. "I presume I *am* addressing Mrs. Audwyn?"

Regina said she was, and sat down opposite her.

"You will forgive me," said Lady Thurston, in a tone that made it quite clear that she considered *she* was the one who ought to be doing the forgiving, "for calling upon you at what appears to be an inopportune moment, Mrs. Audwyn. However, when I was informed by my son that he had made an offer of marriage to a young woman with whom I was quite unacquainted, I naturally felt it to be my duty—regardless of the state of my health, which I may say is far from robust—to come to London immediately. Of course he wished to accompany me, but I preferred to see you alone, and as there were a great many matters that pressingly required his attention at Haddingfield, I prevailed upon him to remain behind. You will, I am sure, comprehend a mother's feelings, Mrs. Audwyn—although I am informed that, though a widow, you have no children of your own?"

Regina, who was by this time able to see clearly how the land lay, said with admirable composure, considering her recent agitation and a steadily rising temper, that she had no children.

"I saw, however," Lady Thurston continued with an air of suspicion, "a young child of some eight or nine years playing with a ball upon the stairs as I entered this house?"

"My young cousin, Giles Stacpoole," Regina said, wondering if Lady Thurston was being deliberately disagreeable or if she actually believed she, Regina, was old enough to have a son nine years of age. "It is his sister I am bringing out this Season."

"Indeed!" said Lady Thurston majestically. "Well, well, that is neither here nor there"—which was the first one of her statements with which Regina was at all inclined to agree. "You will understand, Mrs. Audwyn," Lady Thurston continued, "that it is as a mother that I have come to you—as a mother, I may say, intent upon preserving her son from an act of imprudence that is well calculated to ruin his entire life!" Regina stiffened slightly, but her visitor went on, unheeding, "Indeed, it is difficult for me to credit that my son, who has never before this time caused me so much as a moment's anxiety, should have been led into such folly—"

"I beg your pardon, Lady Thurston," said Regina, who was now sitting very erect, with her head poised on her elegant long neck in a way that would have given warning to anyone who knew her, for in spite of the fragility of her appearance she was not at all fragile in battle, as Lord Wrexam, for one, had already learned. "Am I to understand," she enquired, "that you consider your son's act of becoming affianced to me one of imprudence—I believe you said, even of folly?"

"Precisely!" said the Dowager, speaking so robustly that the forest of plumes upon her bonnet nodded vigorously in sympathy. "My dear Mrs. Audwyn, I have come here to speak plainly to you and whatever it costs me" (or *me,* Regina thought rebelliously), "I am prepared to do so. Surely even *you* must be able to see that for *my* son, Thurston of Haddingfield, with his splendid fortune and undeniable personal endowments, to marry a penniless widow is *quite* unthinkable!"

"As to my being a widow," said Regina, who was rapidly descending into that state of gloriously unself-conscious indignation where one does not in the least care what one says so long as one can score a point off one's opponent by saying it, "you, Lady Thurston, of all people, must agree with me, I am sure, that there is no disgrace attached to that estate. As to my being penniless—which I assure you is a *quite* exaggerated account of my modest income—by your own statement, Sir Mark is already possessed of such an ample fortune that he has no need to consider fortune in choosing a wife. *And,*" she continued ruthlessly, as Lady Thurston, her face rapidly assuming a high flush, showed signs of being about to burst into speech again before she had finished, "as to his being Thurston of Haddingfield, I really am not aware that there is anything in *my* birth or background that might prevent me from accepting the suit even of a gentleman of that exalted station!"

By this time Lady Thurston's face was quite purple and it was obvious that she would have said, "Insolent girl!" or something of the sort, like a character in a melodrama, except that she was not quite stupid enough to believe that it would serve any good purpose. So she smiled instead, with a rather terrifying attempt at archness, and said, "Tut-tut, my dear, we need not quarrel, I think! I am sure, from what Mark has told me, that you are a young woman of sense—far more experienced, I daresay, than my poor boy, who has been so tied to Haddingfield by my precarious state of health that he has had little opportunity to study the world's ways! Indeed, when he made that unfortunate plan of his of going abroad this past winter, I was quite sure what would come of it. 'Depend upon it,' I said to him, 'you will meet some quite unsuitable young woman there who will entangle you in an attachment from which *I* shall be obliged to extricate you, someone who is not in the least the sort of person with whom you, with your attachment to a simple country life, ought to form an alliance—'"

"Oh," said Regina, whose indignation had now taken the form of a fixed resolve not to let Lady Thurston triumph over her by wresting from her the information that she had not the slightest intention of marrying Sir Mark, "I am so very glad to hear you say that, Lady Thurston, since I, too, am much attached to country life! Indeed, I daresay Mark and I shall agree upon spending the greater part of the year at Haddingfield when we are married!"

She then wondered if she had gone mad, and saw by the expression upon Lady Thurston's face that it might have been better for her if she had, for that redoubtable female, who was obviously quite determined to hold Haddingfield and Sir Mark for herself against all comers, seemed to be preparing to bring up her big guns and, in the words of the Bard, cry havoc and let slip the dogs of war.

Unfortunately for her plans, at that moment Hughes appeared to announce the Comte de Chelles. It would have been difficult for Regina to imagine, a half hour before, a situation in which she would have welcomed a visit from M. Jobin, but it was certain that she was glad to see him now, since obviously it was impossible for Lady Thurston to mount a proper attack upon her while he was in the room. Equally obviously, it was impossible for Jobin to enter upon a discussion of the diamonds while Lady Thurston was present—"and as they can't both," her distracted thoughts ran, "outstay the other, I shall be rid of one of them, at least."

And she found herself wishing that Jobin's determination would exceed the Dowager's, which, on the whole, she was inclined to think it would.

They all then made laboured conversation for a period of perhaps ten minutes, during which Jobin glared at Lady Thurston and Lady Thurston glared back at him in such a belligerent fashion that Regina thought hopefully they might begin to quarrel with each other instead of with her. And then the door opened again upon the hall, which now seemed to be inhabited by a large grove of potted palms moving steadily up the stairs to the ballroom like Birnam wood coming to Dunsinane, and Hughes entered to announce, "Lord Wrexam!"

"Good!" thought Regina, in great relief. "I shall contrive to tell him to stay longer than either of them, and then I shall be rid of them both."

And she greeted him with such cordiality that Wrexam, unaccustomed to so much civility from her, raised his black brows at her rather quizzically. His eyes then lighted upon Lady Thurston, and a gleam came into them that Regina instantly felt boded her no good.

"Ah! Lady Thurston!" he said, crossing the room and bowing over the Dowager's hand. "You have come to offer your felicitations, I see!"—which speech, as Lady Thurston's face looked as far from a desire to felicitate anyone on anything as it was possible for a human countenance to do, confirmed all Regina's forebodings concerning Wrexam's malevolent intentions.

Lady Thurston, however, evidently decided that the best way to deal with this remark was to put on the arch air she had tried out on Regina, and, wagging one stout finger at Wrexam, she said playfully that he mustn't believe all he heard and there was many a slip twixt the cup and the lip.

"Exactly my own sentiments," Wrexam said, as he seated himself comfortably beside her. "As I was saying to my old friend, Madame du Grandjean, only yesterday— You are acquainted with Madame du Grandjean, I believe, Comte?" he interrupted himself to enquire.

The false Comte said hastily, "*Mais certainement! Certainement!*"—and added with equal haste and a look of alarm that his health was so poor that he went about very little in society and must now take his leave of them. This he immediately proceeded to do, assuring Regina in a baleful undertone, as he bowed over her hand, that he would call upon her again on the following day.

Regina was so relieved to see him go that she cast an almost friendly glance upon Wrexam, but any feelings of cordiality were immediately dispelled when his lordship turned once more to Lady Thurston and remarked with an appearance of some gravity that he knew long engagements were not much in the mode these days, but that in his experience they were often quite a good idea.

"Don't you agree with me, Lady Thurston?" he asked.

The Dowager, who looked as if she would have liked to say the longer the better, cast a tentatively approving glance upon him and remarked primly that in *her* experience young people were too prone to rush into matrimony without sufficient consideration of its responsibilities.

"Which I am afraid has been the case with my own poor impetuous boy," she said, "as I have just been telling Mrs. Audwyn. One cannot but wish that he had consulted his mother before taking a step of such importance!"

Wrexam immediately said that if *he* had a mother, which unfortunately he had not, as she had been dead since he was three, he would certainly consult her on the matter of choosing a bride.

"And quite right," said Lady Thurston, this time with definite approval in her tone. "I often think that our forebears, in the good old days, had the proper ideas about marriage. My dear papa was used to tell me that he had been entirely guided by his family in making his choice, and though *I* was the only offspring of the match, I cannot but think it was a fortunate one. To be sure, he and dear mama did not always agree, but I am happy to say that, when necessary, she was always able to bring him to a sense of the error of his ways."

"An invaluable attribute in a wife, certainly," Wrexam said judiciously. "But a quality in which I fear Mrs. Audwyn—if she will forgive me for saying so—may be somewhat lacking. Would you say, Lady Thurston—looking at it from a purely practical point of view—that Mrs. Audwyn possesses the ideal qualifications for a wife for Sir Mark? You *will* forgive my speaking so frankly, I am sure."

Lady Thurston, now actually beaming upon him, said she most assuredly would, and that in her opinion it was precisely a lack of frankness upon such occasions as this that was responsible for most of the unfortunate marriages one saw being entered into every day.

"My own idea for Mark, you must know, Lord Wrexam," she confided to him, "is quite a young, docile girl whom I shall be able to form and guide in her wifely duties. With *my* knowledge of life and of my own dear boy's character, I shall be able to instruct her as to exactly how she had best go on, and I am sure that if she is guided by *me*, all will go well!"

"An excellent plan, ma'am!" Wrexam agreed, with a glinting glance from under his eyelids at Regina. "I daresay, in point of fact, you already have some particular young lady in mind?"

"Actually—yes!" Lady Thurston said. "She is a young neighbour of ours in Kent, a considerable heiress, and precisely the sort of biddable girl—"

But Regina had had quite as much of this conversation as she could endure, and in some dudgeon reminded her visitors that, in spite of Lady Thurston's enthusiasm for this paragon, Sir Mark had proposed to *her*.

"Yes, I know. I heard him," Wrexam said soothingly. "But I am sure he will think better of it in time, once Lady Thurston has been able to point out to him the advantages of seeing things as she does."

And he sat looking at her in such a self-satisfied way that she longed to box his ears, which she was prevented from doing only by her higher feelings and the irruption of Mrs. Spear, the housekeeper, into the room, almost in tears, with the dire news that the man from Gunter's was insisting he had not been instructed to provide ices for the evening and was about to depart without promising anything whatever as to their appearance in Cavendish Square.

"Is he, indeed!" said Regina, glad to have someone on whom she might legitimately let loose the thunderbolts of her pent-up wrath.

And, with scant apology to Lady Thurston and Wrexam, she swept out of the room, and might shortly have been heard dealing so effectively with the man from Gunter's that he cravenly turned cat in pan and promised her as many ices as she desired.

When she returned to the library a few minutes later, she found Wrexam there alone.

"Where is Lady Thurston?" she demanded, facing him with a militant flush of victory still on her face.

Wrexam, who had been glancing through the latest of Sir Walter Scott's novels, put it down in a leisurely fashion.

"I sent her away," he said. "Didn't you want me to?"

"Sent her away!"

"Why, yes. Oh, in the most diplomatic way possible, of course. I succeeded in conveying the idea to her, you see, that I am an old friend of the family who exerts a great deal of influence upon you, and that if she would only allow me a free field with you I would do my possible to attempt to convince you that you really don't wish to marry Sir Mark, after all."

Regina gazed at him, almost speechless with indignation.

"*That,*" she said after a moment, "is one of the most abominable, deceitful—"

"Oh, come now!" said Wrexam reasonably. "You really wouldn't rather have had me let that female brimstone have another go at you, would you? I could see your feathers were all on end already when I walked into the room! I should think you would be grateful to me for ridding you of such a precious pair of visitors."

"Well, I *am* grateful to you for frightening the Comte— M. Jobin—away again," Regina admitted. "But it is the outside of enough when you attempt to interfere in my private affairs, Lord Wrexam! What possible concern can it be of yours if I marry Sir Mark Thurston?"

"Ah, but *are* you going to marry him?" asked Wrexam, quite unfairly turning the question back at her. She did not reply, looking at him with a darkling gaze. "I thought not," said his lordship tranquilly, which of course was enough to cause her to say hastily and pertinaciously, "Yes, I am!"

"Coming it a bit too thick and rare, my dear girl!" said Wrexam, looking amused. "And, if I may say so, you are being a bit addlebrained, as well. Why not let that atrocious female extricate you from the bumblebath you have got yourself into?"

"Because I don't *wish* to be extricated!" Regina said, digging the pit she had fallen into a few inches deeper. "I *won't* be extricated! I shall marry Sir Mark if I choose, and neither you nor Lady Thurston can prevent me!"

"Will you take a wager on that?" Wrexam asked in an interested tone, which final bit of impudence so incensed her that she told him to go away at once because she was busy—a statement that was immediately confirmed by Hughes's coming in to inform her that she had best go upstairs at once to the ballroom, because the florist was intent upon placing his potted palms just where the orchestra must sit, and the pantry-boy, who had been set to polishing the lustres on the chandeliers, had broken half a dozen of them and must be dismissed or Mrs. Spear would infallibly go mad.

CHAPTER 13

But by nine o'clock the ballroom, from its beautiful coved ceiling to its mirror-polished floor, stood waiting for the arrival of the first guests in a state of serene expectancy that quite belied the turmoil that had reigned in it a few hours before. The great chandeliers, their lustres reflecting the flicker of hundreds of candles in changing glints of azure and fire-red and gold, brilliantly illuminated the long narrow panels of ormolu on an ivory background that decorated the walls, and the exquisite filigree of the plasterwork Robert Adam had lavished upon ceiling and doorways. Beyond, the graceful curve of the staircase, a circular ascent with an elegant iron balustrade twined into tulip curves, stood equally silent, awaiting the first tread of entering guests, the first ripple of laughter and tumult of voices that would mark the beginning of the ball.

Regina, standing at the head of the second-storey flight in the elegantly simple gown of blossom crape she had chosen for the occasion, experienced, despite her several years in Society, the magic feeling of expectancy that sometimes comes before a ball has become a commonplace, and was conscious of an oddly exciting conviction that something of importance was about to happen.

Seldom was a premonition more promptly justified. She had scarcely turned from her last critical survey of the ballroom, with the intention of visiting Bella's chamber, where her maid was putting the finishing touches upon her young cousin's toilette, when there was a rush of footsteps from above and Giles and Maria surged down from the nursery in their nightgear, with Nannie labouring more deliberately in the rear.

"They *would* come down to see you and Lady Arabella in your ball-gowns, Miss Regina," Nannie said, in the voice of one perilously restraining an exasperation that threatened at any moment to burst the bounds of her control over it.

"*And* the ballroom," Maria proclaimed. She peered inside, drawing in her breath reverentially over glitter and colour and perfume. "It beats Bellacourt all to sticks," she proclaimed. "Something *always* goes wrong at Bellacourt at the last minute. Once Aunt Em had everything draped in yards and yards of pink silk and it caught on fire—"

"Well, nothing is going to catch on fire here, so come along to bed now," Nannie said severely. "Master Giles, give me that dirty old ball. No more play for you tonight."

"But we haven't seen Bella's gown yet," Maria objected, turning to survey with great appreciation Regina's blossom crape robe, and the Denmark satin slippers, long French kid gloves, pearl drops and necklet, and ivory-brisé fan that completed her cousin's toilette.

And Giles, who cared no more for ball-gowns than he did for ballrooms, seconded her loyally: "Yes, we *must* see Bella."

He held on to his ball pertinaciously as Nannie attempted to take it from him; the next moment it parted abruptly into two halves between them and something heavy and glittering slid slowly from it onto the carpet below. It lay there, a coruscating heap of brilliance under the lights of the candelabra above, while Regina and Nannie, Giles and Maria, stared at it in utter silence.

"By—Jupiter!" said Giles, making the first recovery. He squatted on the floor and picked up the flashing heap, which trailed from his fingers in a long wavering circle of what seemed to Regina's dazzled eyes the largest and most brilliant diamonds she had ever seen in her life, strung together upon an antique filigree chain. "By Jupiter!" he repeated, pleased with the grown-up sound of the words. "What is it, Reggie?"

Regina felt as if a rocket had suddenly exploded in her mind, sending out showers of fragmentary thoughts that whizzed through her brain like a dizzying succession of coloured sparks. *The Chelles necklace, of course—it* can't *be, but it is—in a child's ball—in this house—but how—?*

She said to Giles, in what sounded even to her a very odd voice, "Give it to me, Giles, if you please."

"Yes, but what *is* it, Reggie? And how did it get into my ball?" Giles asked, handing the necklace to her readily enough.

"It's a diamond necklace, of course," said Maria scornfully. "Anyone can see *that!*"

Regina, still holding the necklace in one hand, bent down and with the other picked up one of the halves of the gilt ball from which it had so incredibly appeared. It was not, she saw when she examined it, a ball at all, but a hollow replica of an apple, made of wood and painted with gilt, very dirty now and with the gilt flaking off in some places.

I have seen this before, the thought came into her mind; but at the moment she had no notion where.

"Where did you get this, Giles?" she asked, rather helplessly.

Giles, who had lost interest in diamonds and was seeing if he could insert his head between the stair-posts, said he had found it in his toy-box, and was at once snatched away from the peril of becoming a permanent fixture in the hall, at least until the staircase could be dismantled, by Nannie.

"You found it in your toy-box? But who gave it to you?" Regina persisted distractedly. "Someone must have—"

At this point Nannie, who seemed to regard the appearance of the diamonds as something in the nature of a conjurer's trick perpetrated by Giles, with which she was prepared to deal severely, remarked that that toy-box of Master Giles's was a perfect disgrace, and that if he had ever thrown anything away out of it since the day he was born she, Nannie, had never heard of it.

"And as for that ball, Miss Regina," she said, "all I can say is I found it in Master Colin's pocket the day he got that nasty knock on the head—*not* that anyone has ever explained to me what he was doing in Upper Wimpole Street and it's not my business to ask, so I don't know. I was emptying out his pockets before I pressed the coat, and I found this in one of them and naturally I thought it belonged to Master Giles—"

"Naturally," said Regina, still feeling quite dazed.

"—so I took it away and put it in his toy-box," Nannie continued inexorably. "Which I wouldn't have thought it was *his* ball at all, as old and dirty as it was, if it wasn't like pulling teeth to get him to part with anything he's ever owned, as well you know, Miss Regina. And when he has a nice new ball, too, that his lordship gave him before he went off to Mexico—"

"You found the ball in Colin's pocket," Regina repeated, doggedly piecing together in her mind the bits of information she had been able to gather from Nannie's rather incoherent account, "on the day he was attacked in Upper Wimpole Street. And you put it in Giles's toy-box. Really, Nannie! Didn't you think to ask Colin where he had got it?"

"In the state he was in—me ask him about a dirty old ball?" Nannie said incredulously. "All I thought about it was, he's been playing with Master Giles again and picked up one of his balls and put it into his pocket, and him growing so particular, too, about the fit of his coat these days that you'd think he'd take better care—"

"Yes, but if he didn't get it from Giles, where *did* he get it?" Regina demanded.

And then suddenly, as if a curtain had lifted somewhere in her mind, she heard Colin's voice saying, "I was in the drawing room, looking over that rum fireplace—the one with the carved figures of Paris and Venus—to see if the diamonds could have been hidden there," and she saw, in a flash of illumination, the ornate chimney piece in the drawing room of the house in Upper Wimpole Street and the caryatids supporting it, Paris presenting a gilt apple to a simpering Venus—

"Good heavens!" she ejaculated faintly. "The apple! But why didn't he *tell* us he had taken it—?" Nannie looked at her suspiciously. "No, I haven't run mad, Nannie!" Regina said. "But I must see Colin at once! Is he in his bedchamber?"

"In his bedchamber but *not* in his bed," said Nannie grimly. "It was as much as I could do to keep him from dressing and putting in an appearance at the ball tonight, if you'll believe it, Miss Regina, because he'd heard that young Mr. Crowcroft was coming and he wanted to have a talk with him. But I soon put a stop to *that.*"

Which Regina was aware she was quite capable of doing, if she had to carry off his much-prized and newly acquired evening clothes and hide them in the attic, and, feeling grateful for perhaps the hundredth time for Nannie's practically perfect control over the strong wills and unpredictable inclinations of the young Stacpooles, she put the necklace into her reticule and went off to Colin's bedchamber to seek further enlightenment from him concerning it.

She found him wearing a gorgeous brocade dressing gown which he evidently considered the sort of thing favoured by the dandy set, and reading the *Weekly Dispatch* with the bored air of a man of fashion.

"I—say!" he remarked, as Regina walked into the room and he took in the effect of her elegant ball-gown. "You are looking as fine as ninepence this evening, Reggie! Is this all for Sir Mark?"

"As far as I know," Regina said tartly, "Sir Mark is still in Kent, and *don't* play off your airs and graces for me this evening, Colin, for I promise you I am *not* in the mood for it! *Why* didn't you tell me you had found the Chelles diamonds, you abominable boy? I have never had such a shock in my life as when I learned you had brought them here!"

"*I* brought them here? The Chelles diamonds?" Colin looked at her in obvious amazement. "What *are* you talking about, my dear girl?" he demanded. "*I* was the one who was hit over the head, but I think it is you who've gone queer in your attic!"

"I have *not* gone queer in my attic!" Regina said, with some asperity. She drew the necklace from her reticule. "Here *are* the diamonds, and why you did not tell me they were in the ball you brought back from Upper Wimpole Street I simply cannot begin to imagine! I suppose it *was* really the gilt apple from the drawing-room chimney piece—?"

She broke off, observing suddenly that the expression upon Colin's face, as he looked at the sparkling, flashing gems in her hand, was one that could only be described as dumbfounded.

"Good—Lord!" he said slowly, after a moment. "Good Lord, yes! The golden apple! I remember now," he went on, his eyes kindling with excitement as he looked up abruptly into Regina's face. "I was running my hands over the chimney piece—yes, that's it!—trying to see if there was a spring or a catch somewhere that might make it swing open—you remember, Reggie, the way the one did in the castle in *The Midnight Terror,* and they found the skeleton behind it—"

"No, I don't remember because I haven't read it!" Regina said. "And what happened then?"

"Well, the apple simply came off in my hands!" Colin replied, his enthusiasm mounting as he continued his story. "I mean, it fitted into a sort of groove, and I thought it—the groove, that is—might be where the secret catch was, so I dropped the apple into my pocket—at least, I suppose that's what I must have done, though I don't really remember doing it—and set to exploring the groove. And *that* was when I was hit on the head, and when I came to I never thought of the apple, or that I hadn't put it back in place. Good Lord!" he said again, gazing at the diamonds with a kind of blissful awe. "Do you mean they were inside it all the time? But what happened to it after I'd carried it home—?"

"Nannie found it in your pocket and thought it was one of Giles's balls that you had picked up, so she put it in his toy-box," Regina said. "And Giles was playing with it only a few minutes ago, and she tried to take it from him and it came apart—"

"So *that's* why the housebreaker went to Giles's room!" Colin said triumphantly. "He saw me put the apple in my pocket and knocked me unconscious so he could get a look at it; only then Barny came in and he had to hedge off. So he came back here later to look for it—"

"Finding the kitchen window conveniently open, as the hall-boy had left it, and knowing in advance exactly where to look for what he was after," Regina said, and then brought herself up short as the sound of carriage wheels from the street below signalled the arrival of what was no doubt the first of her guests. "Good heavens, I must go downstairs at once!" she said. "People are beginning to arrive. But what on earth shall I do with these—?"

She looked at the diamonds, which she still held in her hand.

"Leave them with me," Colin suggested promptly. "*I'll* see they are kept safe!"

But Regina, with a mistrustful glance at him, said she would rather keep them herself, at least while the ball went on, as it was not likely anyone would attempt to take them from her in the midst of all that company.

She therefore put the necklace back into her reticule and hurried off down the stairs, arriving at the head of the second-storey flight just in time to see Lord Wrexam walking up the stairs in a leisurely fashion.

"Oh, it is you!" she exclaimed, with a feeling of great relief. "How very glad I am to see you!"

"Really?" said Wrexam, raising one eyebrow at her. "I must say, you quite amaze me, Mrs. Audwyn. I believe you did not actually go so far as to tell me you never wished to see me again on the occasion of our last meeting, but I gained the distinct impression—"

"Oh, *do* stop being satirical and *listen* to me, Wrexam!" Regina said impatiently. "The others will be arriving at any moment, and I *must* tell you what has happened!"

She dragged him into the empty ballroom, where, at the far end, the musicians had just taken their places and were beginning to tune their instruments, and hastily proceeded to unfold to him the history of the discovery of the diamonds.

"And what I am to do with them now I have not the least notion!" she said. "Of course if the Comte really *was* the Comte, and not an imposter, I could give them to *him,* but I can't do that now, and if Lescot is an imposter, too—"

"Lescot an imposter?" Wrexam and Regina turned as Bella's astonished voice sounded behind them. She stood in the doorway, a charming little figure in her ball-gown of orange-blossom sarsnet, a length of silver net drapery caught up over her elbows. "What on earth can you mean?" she demanded, a flush beginning to rise in her cheeks.

Regina looked helplessly at Wrexam.

"We had best tell her the whole of it, I expect," he said coolly, "since she has heard so much. You see, my dear Bella, we have known for some two days now that the man who introduced himself to you as the Comte de Chelles is not the Comte at all, but one Jobin, the Comte's former agent, and the question is now an open one as to whether young Lescot is not Lescot, either, but Jobin's accomplice, one of his fellow-servants—"

"Gervais—a servant! Nonsense! You must be all about in your head to think such a thing, Alistair!" Bella said, the flush in her cheeks suddenly mounting vividly. "It isn't possible—!"

"Unfortunately, it is quite possible," Wrexam said dryly. "And since the Chelles diamonds now appear to have fallen into your cousin's hands, it also becomes a matter of considerable importance." He turned to Regina. "By the bye, where have you put the necklace?" he enquired. "In some safe place, I profoundly hope?"

"I haven't had time to put it anywhere," Regina said, rather defensively. "All this has only just happened, you see. I still have it here—"

She opened her reticule, and Wrexam, turning his back upon the musicians to block their view of what he was doing, took the necklace out briefly and examined it. After a moment he said abruptly, "Will you allow me to take charge of this for you?"

"You? Oh, yes!" Regina said, immensely relieved to be rid of the responsibility of protecting the necklace against the wiles of housebreakers and false Comtes; but Bella broke in at once, "No, Reggie! You *can't* give it to *him!* If it is true that the Comte is an imposter, then the diamonds must belong to Mr. Lescot—"

"Ah!" said Wrexam, who was looking at her from under lazily dropped lids. "*Mr. Lescot!* A moment ago it was Gervais, I fancy."

"Well—Gervais, then!" Bella said, facing him with a rather defiant air. "I do think it is stupid to go about calling people *Mr.* This or That when you—when you know them quite well!"

"My unfortunate error," Wrexam said blandly. "I was not aware, you see, that you knew Mr. Lescot—er—*quite well*. My impression was that you had met him for the first time only very recently—"

Bella's cheeks were by this time poppy-red, but she stood her ground determinedly.

"Well, I did—but that makes no difference. He is *not* an imposter!" she said. "Anyone who has ever exchanged half a dozen words with him should know that!"

"Unhappily," Wrexam said, "your cousin and I are not gifted with your unusual powers of discernment, my dear girl. It is also an unfortunate fact that young Lescot appears to bear at least a superficial resemblance to the housebreaker who has been plaguing both Upper Wimpole Street and Cavendish Square—"

Bella's eyes flashed at him dangerously.

"Gervais is *not* a housebreaker!" she said grittily. "*Nor* a thief, *nor* an imposter! He is—he is excessively disagreeable sometimes, and contradicts one in an odiously uncivil way, but he is *not* a criminal, and if you persist in saying he is I shall probably *hit* you!"

She stared furiously at Wrexam, who said in his usual unruffled manner, "Shall you, indeed? But not, I hope, before we have had the quadrille together. You *did* promise it to me, I believe?"

The only reply he received was an angry stamp of a small foot in a white satin sandal; the next moment Bella, in high dudgeon, had run out of the ballroom.

"Well," said Wrexam, looking after her with what Regina could only characterise as a quite imperturbable expression upon his face, "I trust you found that little scene a satisfactory one, Mrs. Audwyn. I mean to say, it *does* give you reason to congratulate yourself upon the success of your stratagems, doesn't it?"

He looked down at her, and Regina found her heart faltering suddenly, though why she could not precisely have said, and could only look back at him enquiringly.

"You *have*," Wrexam said accusingly, "been quite untiring in your efforts to thrust a spoke in the wheel of my determination to marry Bella. It now appears—does it not?—that you may have succeeded. I hope you are suitably gratified."

He spoke in a perfectly collected tone, but Regina, who was not in general given to romantic flights of fancy, wondered all at once if she had broken his heart by her interference—though why the blame should have been hers when nothing she had thus far said and done in the matter appeared to have had the slightest effect upon Bella, she would have found it difficult to say.

"I didn't mean—" she began, in a rather small, self-exculpatory voice.

"Oh yes, you did," Wrexam said inexorably. "You meant it from the start. And when my blighted hopes send me into a rapid decline, I hope you may be sorry, but I daresay you won't. Here come your other guests," he added, and indeed at that moment Hughes's voice was heard announcing, "The Honourable Mr. Frederick Fitzgibbon and Lady Maria Fitzgibbon. Lord and Lady Bascom. Mr. and Mrs. Deliry," and the evening had begun.

CHAPTER

14

It was impossible for Regina, obliged by her role of hostess to stand receiving her guests at the head of the stairs, with feathers, jewels, orders, uniforms, floating draperies, starched white cravats, and satin turbans flowing past her in an endless, bewildering stream, to find an opportunity during the ensuing hour to sort out in any remotely satisfactory manner the violently confused events that had immediately preceded the ball. Fragments of her conversation with Lord Wrexam and Bella in the empty ballroom, visions of the Chelles diamonds glittering on their antique gold chain and of the golden apple that had parted under small, prying fingers to reveal the improbable treasure hidden inside, went jigging through her brain to the accompaniment of the mechanical phrases her tongue kept very properly uttering: "So good of you to come!"—"How nice to see you again!"— "*Enchantée, Madame!*"—"Your Royal Highness is too kind!" Bella, standing beside her, looked charming, excited, and rather mulish, and managed to mutter to her, in one brief lull between arriving guests, "You *must* contrive to get those diamonds back from Alistair! They belong to Mr. Lescot!"

"I shall certainly do nothing of the sort until I am able to find out more about him," Regina, equally *sotto voce*, assured her, and then sank at once into a deep curtsey as a second Royal Duke, stout, bluff, good-humoured Clarence, was announced.

A few moments after the august personage had passed on into

the ballroom Lescot himself was announced. Regina cast a swift glance at her young cousin, half expecting that she might fling herself into the young man's arms or do something of equally Stacpoole-like unconventionality, but beyond saying to him in a quite uncompromising way, "I want to talk to you, Mr. Lescot; I've put you down for the first waltz," she did nothing to bring disgrace upon herself.

Lescot, who looked none too well pleased at having his masculine prerogative of doing the asking reft from him, said, "Very well, Lady Arabella," and bowed to her with a formality that could leave no doubt in her mind of the depth of his disapproval, while Regina thought, in the tiny corner of her mind that was not occupied in noting the hideous puce turban Lady Hamerston was wearing and wondering if the man from Gunter's actually had brought the ices he had promised, "He can't *really* be an imposter, of course. But if he is, and Bella tells him about the diamonds and that Wrexam is carrying them—? I *must* warn Wrexam of that!"

Aloud she said, "Good evening, Mr. Crowcroft. How very nice of you to come!" to that blushing young gentleman, who, quite unable to lower his chin because of his monstrously high shirt-points and elaborately tied cravat, was gazing down his nose at her with an expression of rather owlish alarm upon his face.

"I got your note," he said, having apparently made up his mind to speak at the first opportunity, come what might, because he was quite certain he would go mad if he had to wait about all evening looking for a more proper time. "But I don't think I quite understand it. Delighted to do anything in my power for you, of course—*anything!*" Mr. Crowcroft emphasised, suddenly feeling that he was acting the part of a churl and should be cast into outer darkness for being so stupid. "But what is it, actually, that you want me to do—?"

Regina, casting a hurried glance down the staircase, which Lord and Lady Sefton were now mounting, said it was only that there was a young man at the ball that evening who might possibly be the person he had had the encounter with in the house in Upper Wimpole Street, and would he be so good as to look at all the guests and see if any one of them might be the housebreaker.

She did not dare to be more specific and mention Lescot's name with Bella standing just beside her; but if she had any idea that she could forestall Bella from taking umbrage at her scheme by this manoeuvre she was soon to be disillusioned.

"I think," Bella said indignantly, as soon as Mr. Crowcroft had passed on into the ballroom, "that Mr. Lescot has a right to know the sort of things that are happening here! I intend to tell him all about the diamonds, and about the Comte, and as for Mr. Crowcroft, I shall introduce him to Mr. Lescot myself, because he—I mean Gervais—is *not* the housebreaker—"

"Hush!" said Regina imperatively, as she saw Lord and Lady Sefton now upon them. And, to her approaching guests, "Lady Sefton, how good of you to come! My lord—"

It was half an hour later before she was able to leave her post at the head of the stairs and go into the ballroom, where by that time the dancing was in full swing. She at once looked for Bella, who had escaped a few minutes before, saying she was quite certain no one else was coming and at any rate they were playing a waltz and she had promised the first one to Mr. Lescot. Regina found her, as she had feared, not only dancing with young Lescot but talking sixteen to the dozen to him. She made a gesture of exasperation and at the same moment found Lord Wrexam at her elbow.

"Hello!" he said placidly. "What is it now? Haven't the ices arrived, after all?"

"Oh," she said, turning a vexed and slightly alarmed face upon him, "as if I could care at this moment if there wasn't an ice or a lobster patty in the house! Look at Bella! She has promised to tell Mr. Lescot everything about our finding the diamonds and about the Comte's not being the Comte and our suspecting him— I mean Mr. Lescot—of being an imposter, too, and you can see for yourself that that is exactly what she is doing! And if he *is* an imposter, and knows you are carrying the jewels tonight, heaven knows what he may take it into his head to do to get them from you! Perhaps you had best go home at once and lock up your house when you have got there."

"What, and miss all the fun?" Wrexam said. "Not for a hundred guineas, my dear girl."

"But if he knocks *you* on the head—" Regina said, a trifle anxiously.

"He is quite welcome to try. By the bye, I presume you *have* asked young Crowcroft to see if he is able to identify Lescot as the man he saw in Upper Wimpole Street? He—that is, Crowcroft—has been dodging about the ballroom in such a peculiar manner, looking like an apprentice Bow Street Runner with suspicions, that I made sure you must have done so."

"Oh yes, I have," Regina said. "Where is he now?" She broke off to say, as she was interrupted by a compliment upon the success of the ball from Lady Jersey, passing at the moment, "Oh, Lady Jersey, how kind of you to say so!"

"And you, Wrexam," Lady Jersey continued, tapping his arm with her fan as she gave him a teasing smile, "of course one was certain to find *you* here tonight!" She looked from him to Regina and back again. "How does your suit progress? One hears the most alarming rumours of a rival!"

"Sir Mark Thurston?" Wrexam said calmly. "My dear Sally, surely you cannot have such a poor opinion of Mrs. Audwyn as to believe she has no more discrimination than *that!*"

Lady Jersey laughed and passed on, and Wrexam said amiably, "Detestable woman. She'll make mischief any time she can if she isn't stopped. Now, let me see, where were we—?"

"You can't stop *me*," Regina said, lifting her chin, "from marrying Sir Mark by making unkind remarks about him, Lord Wrexam. And if you mean to imply that I ought to prefer *you* to him—"

"—I have a supremely faulty sense of values," Wrexam finished it for her, with aplomb. "But I'm rather afraid I do, you know. Besides, I don't think you would like being married to him."

"I should like it," Regina said pertinaciously, "a great deal better than being married to *you!*"

"Now there," Wrexam said judiciously, "I rather fancy you are wrong. But since, as it says in the old song, 'Nobody asked you to,' I fear the question must remain moot. Shall we return to Mr. Crowcroft? I rather think you should hunt him up and see what he has to say about young Lescot; he must have had ample opportunity to examine him by this time."

"Yes, but, you see, he doesn't know it is Mr. Lescot he is meant to examine," Regina said, her attention successfully diverted from her indignation with him by this return to the troublesome matter of Lescot's identity. "I only told him to see if he thought any of the guests looked like the housebreaker he had seen in Upper Wimpole Street—"

"Good God! He has probably run mad by this time trying to carry out *that* assignment," Wrexam said impolitely. "Did *you* ever try to examine four hundred people—make it two hundred, granting him the wit to exclude the females, which by your description I'm not sure he has—for a resemblance to a stranger you'd seen only once in your life, and that under rather trying circumstances?"

Regina was about to defend herself by saying that she hadn't dared mention Lescot's name to Mr. Crowcroft in Bella's presence, but reflecting that this could not but bring to Wrexam's mind the sudden preference for the young Frenchman that Bella had displayed just before the ball, she held her tongue. After all, she thought uncomfortably, it *was* possible that she had mistaken Wrexam's feelings, well camouflaged as they were behind that witty, imperturbable mask of the man of the town, and that he really was seriously attached to her young cousin. And she remembered, with a quite unaccountable sensation of hollowness somewhere inside her, Wrexam's reply to her a few days before when she had enquired what he knew of ardent love—"More than you think, my child. More than you think!"

"If he really *is* in love with her, then it is all quite different from Etienne and me and I have no right to try to keep them apart," she thought, with that horrid, empty feeling inside her growing even more pronounced. "Only perhaps she is not in love with *him*—Oh, dear! What a tangle!"

But she had no opportunity to cogitate on the matter further, for at that moment Mr. Crowcroft, who had apparently espied her entering the ballroom, was seen making a determined and perspiring way towards her across the room.

"Here is Mr. Crowcroft now," she said hurriedly to Wrexam.

"Mr. Crowcroft," she went on, as he came within earshot, "you are exactly the person I most wished to see! Have you found anyone—?"

Mr. Crowcroft, apparently about to reply, suddenly brought himself up short with a harried glance at Wrexam.

"Oh—this is Lord Wrexam, and you need not mind him," Regina said kindly. "He knows all about everything."

Mr. Crowcroft looked as if that was more than he did, but he politely refrained from saying so, and remarked instead with an unhappy air that he had looked at everyone he could, but up to the present moment had seen no one whom he would be willing to identify as the man he had had the tussle with in Upper Wimpole Street.

"What about this young man?" Wrexam asked, nodding towards Lescot, who, as the music ended, was seen to be approaching them under Bella's purposeful guidance. The young Frenchman was looking rather pale and, Regina thought, more than a little discomposed—in fact, quite angry.

Bella, however, gave him no opportunity to speak as they came up, for she said at once, with her Stacpoole lack of consideration for the fact that every word she spoke might be overheard, "Mr. Crowcroft, this is Mr. Lescot. Is *he* the man you saw attacking Colin in Upper Wimpole Street?"

It would have been difficult to say which of the two young men placed in confrontation with each other by this ruthlessly direct question was the more embarrassed. Lescot turned white and Mr. Crowcroft scarlet, and the latter's eyes, after a hunted glance at Lescot, went in anguished appeal to Regina.

"Really, Bella, this is quite outrageous of you!" Regina said, feeling equally for both the young men.

Lescot began to say something in a low, vehement voice; the words collided with a stammering utterance from Mr. Crowcroft, and both fell abruptly silent.

"I rather think," Wrexam's equable drawl relieved the tension of the instant, "that a more private setting for this conversation might be advisable, Mrs. Audwyn. As I recall, there is a very convenient little anteroom just behind us—"

"Oh, yes!" said Regina thankfully. "Do let us go there. Mr. Crowcroft—"

Mr. Crowcroft looked as if he would much rather have bolted out to the stairs and thence out of the house, never to darken its doors again, but Wrexam's hand was on his elbow, guiding him inexorably into the anteroom. It was a small room, really little more than an alcove, with a pair of thin-legged chairs, a yellow satinwood sofa, and a pier glass over an inlaid Buhl table its only articles of furniture. Everyone looked at the chairs and the sofa but no one sat down.

"Now," said Wrexam, who seemed by mutual consent to have been elected moderator, "suppose we get on with it. Crowcroft, if you will give us your opinion as to whether Mr. Lescot was the man you saw in Upper Wimpole Street, I believe we shan't be obliged to trouble you further."

He looked enquiringly at Mr. Crowcroft, who cast another hunted glance at Lescot and said something inaudible.

"We can't understand you," Bella said loudly and impatiently. "Can't you speak up?"

"He—he isn't. At least I don't think so. I'm very nearly s-sure," Mr. Crowcroft said hoarsely, running a finger desperately under his elaborate cravat, much to the detriment of its starched folds.

"There! Do you hear that?" Bella said. She looked triumphantly at Wrexam. "Of course it wasn't Gervais!"

Wrexam, politely ignoring her, said to Mr. Crowcroft, "You are not prepared, I take it, to make a more positive statement?"

Mr. Crowcroft said miserably that he was *almost* sure. "I only saw him for a moment before he came at me, you see," he said. "Deuced hard to get a look at a fellow while you're having a turn-up with him. But I don't *think*—Of course, he *did* have black hair—"

He cast another doubtful glance at Lescot.

"This," said Lescot suddenly, "is intolerable!" He was still very pale, but there was a look of furious resolution upon his face. "If it is my word, my honour, that is being impugned," he said, "I must ask for satisfaction from both of you gentlemen—"

"Oh, for heaven's sake!" said Regina, losing her temper completely at this display of masculine inability to resolve a difference of opinion except by recourse to arms. "If there is any talk of a duel between any of you, I warn you I shall take those tiresome diamonds and throw them into the Thames! No one is impugning your honour, Mr. Lescot, but you *must* see that until we are satisfied that you really are who you say you are—as the Comte most certainly is not—we cannot give the diamonds to you!"

Lescot, looking very stiff and Gallic, said that under no circumstances whatever would he take the diamonds, at any rate, as they belonged to his uncle, the Comte de Chelles.

"But he *isn't* the Comte!" Regina said, at which point Wrexam remarked that Mr. Crowcroft, who was by this time quite goggle-eyed with incomprehension, might well be allowed to return to the ballroom, as it appeared there was no further contribution he could make to this interesting conversation.

"I rather think," he added, with a kindly air, "that it would be best if you considered the entire matter one of the strictest confidence, Crowcroft. I can answer for my own pacific intentions, you see, if it should chance to be bruited about, but not entirely for Mr. Lescot's."

Mr. Crowcroft, being, as Colin had stated, a well-plucked 'un, was heard to state here, in a rather muffled voice and with a very red face, that of course he wouldn't say anything, but not because he was afraid of anything anyone might do, which made Regina almost push him out of the room before hostilities could erupt all over again.

"And *now*," said Bella, who had obviously been awaiting her opportunity to re-enter the conversation, "*will* you give the necklace to Mr. Lescot, Alistair? You heard Mr. Crowcroft say he wasn't the housebreaker."

"Which doesn't precisely prove, however—does it?—that he really *is* Lescot," Wrexam said pleasantly. He looked at the young Frenchman. "I suppose you might be the one to help us out here," he said. "No doubt you can produce some suitable identification—?"

Lescot, who was still looking shaken and at the same time so unwontedly fierce that even Bella seemed a little awed, said with an air of icy hauteur that he was not accustomed to having his word doubted, and it seemed more to the point to him at the present moment for them to inform *him* upon what evidence they based their preposterous statement that the man known as the Comte de Chelles was not really his uncle.

"Well, we don't exactly say *that*, you know," Regina said scrupulously. "That he isn't your uncle, that is, because after all he may be. But he certainly isn't the Comte de Chelles. We think he is probably a man named Jobin, who was the Comte's agent. Madame du Grandjean, who knew them both but of course hasn't seen either of them for twenty years, thinks that is who he is, at any rate."

Lescot looked rather staggered for a moment by this news, but recovered quickly and asked with an air of contempt if their charges against the Comte were based, then, solely upon the twenty-year-old recollections of a very old woman.

"I have met her, your Madame du Grandjean," he said. "A remarkable lady, I will admit—but memory sometimes plays strange tricks in old minds." He bowed to Regina. "I am sorry, Madame, but I must refuse to believe your allegations against my uncle," he said. "As for those against myself—they are, as I have already said, so insulting that if you were a man I should feel obliged to resent them. I do not know what Lord Wrexam has to do in this matter, but if he—"

"I," said Wrexam, with a gleam of amusement upon his face, "am merely an innocent bystander, I assure you! And you may thirst for my blood all you like, you silly young chub, but you are not likely to get it, whether I go out with you or not. I am a tolerably good shot, you know."

"Don't be condescending, Alistair!" Bella said severely. "We all know you have been out half a dozen times—"

"In my salad days!" Wrexam murmured extenuatingly.

"Yes, I know, but that is probably only because people are afraid to call you out now. Gervais isn't afraid, but I won't have him—"

"Lady Arabella!" Lescot broke in, outraged. "May I ask how this matter concerns you?"—at which moment the orchestra in the ballroom struck up a country-dance, and Wrexam, saying politely to Regina, "Our dance, I believe," led her forthwith out of the anteroom and on to the floor.

"But what are we to do about Mr. Lescot?" she protested, looking back still at the anteroom as he led her into the set.

"Never mind about Mr. Lescot," Wrexam said. "He will be fully occupied in quarrelling with Bella for the next half hour, and when he finally comes to his proper senses again will no doubt depart in high dudgeon with all of us."

"But is he *really* Lescot, do you think?"

"Oh yes, I think so—but not firmly enough to hand over the diamonds to him at this present. The mere fact that he disdains advancing any proof of his identity speaks in his favour there; an imposter would be far more likely to make haste to establish his bona fides. At any rate, I believe I am in the way to finding out something more conclusive about him, and when I have done that, we shall be in a better position to decide what we are to do."

Regina would have liked to discuss the matter with him further, but engaging in a set of country-dances in a crowded ballroom offers little opportunity for private conversation. Unfortunately, when the set was over her attention was claimed by other of her guests, and she did not see Wrexam again until much later, when he took his leave of her. By that time, as he had predicted, Lescot had long since departed, but she was still uneasy about the diamonds, and whispered a warning to Wrexam, between her smiling replies to the good-nights and felicitations of her other guests, to take every precaution not to be waylaid as he was returning home.

"Do you carry a sword-stick?" she demanded. "I know they are rather old-fashioned now, but it would be so very useful to have one upon an occasion like this—"

"Unfortunately not," he said gravely. "But may I say, Mrs. Audwyn, that your solicitude for my safety quite unmans me? I had been under the impression—mistaken, no doubt—that you would have been willing to sacrifice even a fortune in diamonds to have me put out of the way, or should I say, Bella's way?"

"Very well; perhaps I would have—but they are not *my* diamonds!" Regina said, with spirit; and then watched him go out the door with that horrid sinking feeling appearing again most disturbingly inside her. What if he *was* found murdered in some dark doorway in the morning? she thought. That little wretch Bella had no doubt told Lescot all about his having the jewels upon him, and even if Lescot were not the housebreaker, someone certainly was, and might be lying in wait somewhere outside there in the cool misty dawn that was just beginning to break over London.

But she comforted herself presently by recalling one of Bella's tales of Wrexam's prowess in the noble art of self-defence, very improperly wrested by that enterprising young lady from a sporting baronet who was, like Wrexam, a frequent visitor to Gentleman Jackson's famous Boxing Saloon in Bond Street, and decided that if trouble *did* come, his lordship would more probably than not be very well able to take care of himself.

This did not prevent her, however, from attempting to read Bella a lecture on her imprudence when they had both left the deserted ballroom—its flowers wilting now and its myriad candles guttering in the cold unkind light of dawn—and had gone upstairs to bed. It was, she knew, a lost cause to expect Bella to attend to anything she might say at that hour, for her young cousin was yawning herself to pieces, now that the excitement of the ball was over, and showing every intention of falling asleep without preamble in the nearest available chair or bed; but she persisted.

And she had at least the success of seeing Bella's eyes come wide open and stare at her indignantly as she gathered the gist of the reproof that was being made to her.

"You think Gervais—Mr. Lescot—might attack Alistair and take the diamonds from him because he knows he is carrying them?" she said incredulously. "Honestly, Reggie, Gervais isn't—he wouldn't—"

"Are you in love with him?" Regina found herself asking abruptly, and then as abruptly wished she hadn't.

Bella was staring at her blankly. "In love?" she said. "With *Gervais?*" And again, rather helplessly, "Honestly, Reggie—!"

"No, I expect you aren't," Regina said carefully. "I mean to say, you couldn't be, since you are in love with Lord Wrexam—"

Bella interrupted her, her cheeks suddenly flaming scarlet. "I consider that Alistair has behaved abominably!" she said. "And I shall tell him so the very next time I see him. And now I am very tired, Reggie, and I don't at all wish to talk about it any more, and if you don't mind, I am going to bed!"

"And that," said Regina to herself, as Bella flounced into her bedchamber and she went on down the hall to her own, "is that," which as far as she could tell meant nothing at all. But as she was too tired herself at this point to be able to think of any more apt comment on the affairs of the night, she was obliged to let it stand. In the morning, she thought, she would be able to sort things out better and think what she was to do about the hideous tangle into which matters seemed to have fallen—and, so thinking, she got herself to bed, where she fell at once into a deep and dreamless sleep.

CHAPTER
15

She did not awaken until late the next morning, and had her breakfast chocolate in bed to the news that the Comte de Chelles had already called and had promised to return later in the day.

"Oh, dear! Perhaps Mr. Lescot has told him about the diamonds," she thought. "But at least that must mean that Wrexam arrived home with them safely, or the Comte would not trouble to come worrying *me* about them."

She then instructed her Abigail to tell Hughes on no account to admit the Comte if he were to call again, as she had no intention of attempting to deal with him before she had been able to hold a proper conference with Wrexam, and went downstairs to find Bella in the sulks, or as near to them as it was possible for a girl to be who had already received half a dozen bouquets that morning from her admirers of the previous evening.

Among them, of course, there was one from Lord Holt, but Bella, as if determined to make herself as militantly unco-operative as possible, had had one of the footmen carry it up to Colin's room upon the grounds that invalids liked flowers, thus precipitating more disagreeableness, as Colin had refused with great emphasis to have it and had declared himself so far from being an invalid that he intended going to view a badger drawn in a menagerie in Holborn that very morning.

When Regina and Miss Abthorpe between them had at last

succeeded in convincing him of the inadvisability of his undertaking so ambitious a program on his first day out of his bedchamber, Bella continued the disagreeableness by demanding of Regina what she and Wrexam had meant by not turning the Chelles diamonds over to Lescot at once. If the Comte, she said, was actually not the Comte, but an imposter, and the real Comte was dead, then it was plain that Lescot, as his heir, must have every right to the jewels.

"And as far as that goes, if the old Comte is dead, Gervais is the Comte de Chelles himself now, isn't he?" she said—"unless they do things differently in France. Not that I expect that will be of any importance to him, because he is very democratic, and besides, people don't have titles in America. But I am sure the diamonds would fetch a great deal of money if they were sold, and then he could buy more land and enlarge his plantation, which he would like very much to do, I know, because he has told me all about it. And I am *not* in love with him!" she added hastily, as she saw Regina look at her with an expression of sudden misgiving upon her face. She raised her chin. "He—no doubt he is already engaged to his cousin, Miss Grevel," she said, "because he talks about her very often, and says she is very agreeable, though she sounds a horrid prig to me. And, besides, I am going to marry Alistair."

Which statement caused Regina to reflect resignedly that at least Lord Arun would probably consider it better for his daughter to marry Wrexam than a man who might turn out to be an adventurer; but for some reason the reflection gave her very little satisfaction.

She then composed herself to await Wrexam's arrival and the opportunity to discuss further with him what they were to do about the events of the previous evening; but the hours passed and no Wrexam appeared. An impatient message finally despatched by her to his lordship's house brought in reply only the news that his lordship was gone out, and had left no word as to when he might return, which seemed to her to be adding insult to injury. When at last he did put in an appearance at Cavendish Square very late in the afternoon, she told herself that she had half a mind to send down word that she was not at home.

But of course she did nothing of the kind, being far too anxious to hear what he had been doing all day and exceedingly curious, besides, to learn the identity of the person (Hughes, she noted, did not dignify him by the term "gentleman") whom he had brought with him.

The "person" turned out to be a rather frightened-looking little man in a snuff-coloured coat and Angola pantaloons, who looked at her apprehensively as she entered the drawing room, where Hughes had bestowed the visitors, and was at once introduced to her by Wrexam as Mr. Whimster.

"Mr. Whimster," Wrexam explained with a benevolent air, "is the proprietor of a jeweller's establishment in Cranbourn Alley, and has information concerning the Chelles diamonds that I feel will be of particular interest to you."

He looked encouragingly at Mr. Whimster. Mr. Whimster, however, said nothing for the moment, being engaged in burrowing in his coat pocket for a large red handkerchief. Having found it, he drew it out and mopped his forehead with it as though the day were very warm, which it was not, being overcast and coming on to rain.

"Well?" Regina said, feeling quite at a loss as to what information the little man could have to give her about the diamonds, now that they were no longer lost.

Mr. Whimster looked appealingly at Wrexam, but, reading nothing in his face but courteous interest, cleared his throat rather desperately and said in a hoarse voice to Regina, "Well, Missus, you see, it's like this. They're paste."

"*Paste?* The Chelles diamonds?" Regina could not believe her ears. She looked incredulously at Wrexam. "*Paste?* But they *can't* be—!"

"I am sorry, but they can," Wrexam assured her. "The very finest, guaranteed to deceive anyone but an expert. And you needn't take Mr. Whimster's word for it, because Messrs. Rundell and Bridge, who, as you know, are the Regent's jewellers, told me exactly the same thing when I brought the necklace to them this morning. But Mr. Whimster, you see, is even more knowledgeable about the matter than they are, for he has the advantage of being the man who actually made them. I am told he is quite an expert practitioner in his field."

"All on the right side of the Law, Missus!" Mr. Whimster hastened to assure her. "All on the right side of the Law! I put it to you, Missus—if a lady finds she needs the use of a few pounds, temporary like, and don't see her way to asking her husband for it, who's the worse off if she pops a ring or a brooch to get the pitch and pay, and then has a copy of it made so Friend Husband won't twig it's gone? It's legitimate business, Missus; strike me if I've ever touched a job yet that wasn't legitimate business!"

"Yes, but—" Regina looked helplessly from him to Wrexam. "I simply *can't* understand it!" she said. "*Who* had the copy made? You *can't* mean that Etienne—?"

"Stone by stone," said Wrexam, looking amused. "But don't look so tragic, my dear girl; apparently at least part of the proceeds went not for his—er—personal pleasures but for what might be called an altruistic cause. At least it appears, from certain enquiries I have made at the Foreign Office, that very considerable sums were known to have been flowing from some mysterious source to finance a cadre of Bonapartist agents operating in London during the late war—a source that was identified just at the close of the war as being a certain house in Upper Wimpole Street. More," he added, looking at Mr. Whimster, "I cannot say at present, but logic suggests that the necklace must have been the fount from which all this largesse flowed."

Mr. Whimster, who was looking nervous at this talk of wars and foreign agents, here remarked in some alarm that he didn't know anything about any agents and didn't want to, and that if a cove was to turn an honest piece of business, not knowing there was anything rum about it, there wasn't nothing in it he could be taken up for, or there was no justice in the world.

"As to that," Wrexam said equably, "there is very little, I believe, but in this case I can assure you that you are not in the slightest danger. As a matter of fact, you may run along now. My sole reason in bringing you here, you see, was to support my story that the stones are actually paste, my own credit with Mrs. Audwyn being rather lacking."

Mr. Whimster, needing no second invitation, at once took his leave, whereupon Regina, looking rather indignantly at Wrexam, said there was no need for him to have done that, because she certainly would never have thought, even without Mr. Whimster to vouch for him, that he would deceive her in such a matter as this.

"Oh, wouldn't you? I *am* getting on, then," Wrexam said, with a satisfied air. "There has been a time, I believe, when you would not have put murder and arson, not to say simple grand larceny, beyond me—"

Regina said firmly not to be silly, because no matter how badly he had behaved at certain times she had never believed he would do any of those things, and then asked what they were to do about the diamonds.

"I daresay it will make no difference who gets them, if they are only paste," she said. "Only I do think M. Jobin is likely to make difficulties and not believe us in the least when we tell him they are worth nothing, after all."

"Then we shan't tell him," Wrexam said promptly.

"Shan't tell him?"

"Precisely, my child. Let him find out for himself. In other words, let us give him the paste necklace and allow him to leave the country with it, which is no doubt what he will do the moment he has it in his hands. In that way we shall be rid of him *and* the necklace without the least breath of scandal or inconvenience—"

Regina looked rather doubtful. "But when he finds out—?" she said.

"When he finds out he will be in America, or on the Continent, or wherever it is that he has fled to with his ill-gotten gains," Wrexam said, "and I very much doubt that by that time he will be willing to venture another journey to England to try to discover what has become of the real jewels. It was a risky business at best for him to have passed himself off as the Comte here, you know—a fact he is perfectly aware of, I am sure. He did not dare so much as to attempt it, you will remember, until he was assured that your husband was no longer alive."

Regina thought the matter over. Certainly, she thought, there would be a great many advantages in following Wrexam's plan.

They could not expose Jobin, and rid themselves of him in that way, without a scandal, and if they did not turn him over to the authorities they would be obliged to continue to deal with him themselves. And even if they did succeed in convincing him that the necklace that had been hidden in the house in Upper Wimpole Street was made of paste, he might still believe that the real jewels were in their possession as well, and continue his attempts to obtain them by fair means or foul.

"Very well," she said, coming to a decision with her usual promptness. "You are quite right, I think, and we shall give the necklace to M. Jobin. But what about Mr. Lescot? Will he leave the country with him, do you think?"

"Not," said Wrexam, "if Jobin can contrive to give him the slip. Among my other labours during this long and fatiguing day, I may tell you, has been interviewing an American gentleman named Bowser, who deals, I am given to understand, in a large way in cotton. Mr. Bowser is not only well acquainted with young Mr. Lescot, but he is also willing to take his Bible oath, if necessary, that the young man at present going about London under that name is exactly who he claims to be—the nephew of the Comte de Chelles and a pillar of New Orleans society. And as Mr. Bowser, in turn, is vouched for by my own solicitor, a gentleman not inclined to vouch for anything that cannot be proved to his entire satisfaction before a Court of Law, I think we must write off Mr. Lescot as an imposter and a house-breaker. Discreet enquiries by my valet at the Fenton Hotel, I may also inform you, have elicited the information that the bogus Comte has his own valet with him, a *young, active, black-haired man* who appears to spend remarkably little of his time in attendance upon his master, and who comes and goes at the very odd hours that a housebreaker's occupation would seem to require—" He broke off, seeing that Regina was observing him in speechless admiration. "I have dazzled you, no doubt," he said kindly, "by the brilliance of my investigations. Pray think nothing of it. These strokes of genius are common to me."

"Oh, *don't* try to make light of it!" Regina said, her eyes shining with relief and pleasure. "You *have* been terribly, terribly clever, and I am sure it was all a *great* deal of trouble for you, and I am everlastingly grateful! But poor Mr. Lescot! No wonder he was so furious with us last night for thinking *he* was the housebreaker!"

"Yes, but rather a dull sort of fellow not to have seen through Jobin himself, don't you think?" Wrexam asked. "However, do not let us be uncharitable. He is young and no doubt unaccustomed to being approached by oily rogues who have prigged the family papers and portraits and present themselves to him as near relations. We must all learn by experience, as the copybooks say. Now about Jobin—the sooner you can bring him here and we can fob off these baubles upon him the better, I should think."

Regina said she would despatch a message to him at once, and rang for Hughes. Her instructions to him to send one of the footmen around to Fenton's Hotel with an urgent request to the Comte de Chelles to come to Cavendish Square as soon as possible met with the unexpected news, however, that the Comte had just at that moment presented himself upon the doorstep for the third time that day with a demand to see her—"really most insistent upon this occasion," as Hughes put it darkly—and was he therefore to show him in?

"Yes, certainly," said Regina, and in a very few moments Jobin himself, looking exceedingly belligerent and with his penetrating black eyes boring holes into everything they fell upon, marched into the room, evidently prepared for battle and with all flags flying.

"Madame," he began without preamble, "what means this? All day I am kept dancing upon your doorstep—'Madame cannot see you; Madame is gone out.' I now demand—*demand*, Madame—"

"Oh, pray don't demand anything until you have heard what I have to say to you, Comte," Regina said soothingly. "I am sure you have every reason to be upset with all this delay, but everything has been *quite* cleared up now and we have found the necklace, and of course you must have it at once. Lord Wrexam, will you—?"

"By all means," said Wrexam politely, and he drew the necklace from his pocket and presented it to the dumbfounded Jobin.

The false Comte, indeed, was so dumbfounded that for a few moments he did not even reach out his hand to take the jewels.

"*Pardon!*" he stammered at last, his eyes all but starting out of his head at this glittering evidence of roguery rewarded. "*Pour moi?* You wish *me* to have—?"

"But naturally! They are yours, are they not?" Wrexam said affably. "You *can't* mean to say, now, that you thought Mrs. Audwyn wouldn't turn them over to you as soon as she'd found them? Deuced improper of her not to do so; I mean, after all, they *are* yours."

"*Mais certainement! Certainement!* They are mine!" gabbled Jobin, reaching a trembling hand out for the jewels. "A thousand pardons, Madame! A thousand thanks! But where—how—?"

"Oh, it is a very long and complicated story," Regina said hastily, "but they were found in the house in Upper Wimpole Street, just as you predicted. And I can't tell you how happy I am now that the whole affair has at last been brought to an end—"

"Yes, yes! *Mon Dieu,* yes! To an entirely satisfactory end!" exclaimed the false Comte, who was staring at the false diamonds in his hand as if he had been mesmerised by them. Suddenly coming to himself, he began hastily stowing the necklace away in his pocket. "My gratitude," he announced with dramatic fervour, "shall follow you, *chère Madame,* throughout all the days of my life! You have rescued me from penury; you have restored to me the means to live as one of my name and birth should be able to live—"

"Yes," said Wrexam amiably, "I am sure both Madame and I are happy to see you receive your just deserts, Comte. Happens so seldom, you know—poetic justice and all that. Quite a pleasure, I assure you, to see it all working out so nicely. As I was saying to my friend Madame du Grandjean only the other day—You *are* acquainted with Madame du Grandjean, I believe, Comte?"

The false Comte, paling at the name, said that he was indeed, and added hastily that as he had urgent business to attend to, he would now take his leave of them.

"By all means," Wrexam said. "We shall hope to have the pleasure of meeting you again soon"—to which M. Jobin replied cautiously that nothing would give *him* greater pleasure, but unfortunately he had received a communication that very day that made it imperative for him to return to America at once.

"America, eh?" said Wrexam to Regina as M. Jobin walked hurriedly from the room, to the accompaniment of a heavy mutter of thunder from what appeared to be an approaching storm. "I daresay that means he is headed for the Continent. No need to sponge off young Lescot any longer—or at least he will live in that happy delusion until he tries to get rid of that necklace. By the way," he broke off to enquire, "what's that devilish noise going on downstairs? It sounds as if the Revolution had begun in your front hall and your butler was having rather the worst of it."

CHAPTER
16

The Revolution, when they had both succumbed to an un-
dignified curiosity and gone out into the hall to peer over the
bannisters, resolved itself into Lady Thurston apparently having
a fit of hysterics on a cane-backed settee in the hall, with Sir
Mark hovering over her in a state of obviously acute embarrassment, the bogus Comte vainly attempting to obtain his hat
from Hughes, who was equally vainly attempting to succour the
afflicted Lady Thurston, and Bella standing transfixed upon the
lowest step of the staircase.

"Go away! Go away, you unnatural boy!" shrieked the hysteri-
cal Dowager, who had got her head well back and her bonnet
over one eye, and was drumming vigorously with both heels
upon the floor. "Forsake me! Desert me! It is what I should have
expected! What are a mother's claims to a siren's charms? Go—a-
way!"

"Mama, for heaven's sake—!" said the agitated Sir Mark, and,
"My lady, I must beg you to compose yourself!" said Hughes, in
shocked antiphony.

"I should not have guessed," remarked Wrexam in an interested voice, "that Lady Thurston was a devotee of the theatre,
but surely she has never invented all *this* in her own miniscule
brain." He turned to Regina. "Come along, siren," he said. "We
must go down. Surely you won't wish to shirk your own part in
this little drama."

Regina would have liked nothing better than to do exactly that, but as the chatelaine of the house she knew her duty and so accompanied Wrexam reluctantly down the stairs. As she approached the settee, Hughes, desisting from his unavailing efforts to calm the distraught Dowager, turned a disapproving face upon her.

"I fancy, ma'am," he said in the unruffled tones of a veteran who had survived forty years of virtuoso Stacpoole scenes and was not now to be put off his stride by what he obviously considered a mere amateur performance, "that the lady is in a somewhat upset condition owing to the coming storm. I have known many ladies who have become, if I may so express myself, Quite Unmanageable with thunder and lightning in the vicinity. I have taken the liberty of sending Charles for restoratives."

At that moment Charles himself, the second footman, appeared in the hall bearing a tray with a decanter and glasses upon it, closely followed by Mrs. Spear, the housekeeper, carrying a vinaigrette. This she at once waved encouragingly under Lady Thurston's nose, while Sir Mark, having poured brandy with a rather unsteady hand from the decanter that Charles had brought, stood holding the glass helplessly and looking miserably as if he wished he were anywhere but where he was.

"Give it to me," said Regina, who shared his feelings but, being female, was made of sterner stuff in an emotional crisis.

And, taking the glass from Sir Mark's nerveless fingers, she approached Lady Thurston and proffered it to her.

Lady Thurston, opening one eye to glare at her balefully, shuddered and continued to shriek in an alarming manner.

"My hat, please!" M. Jobin's voice was heard to say despairingly in an interval when the Dowager was obliged to stop to draw breath; but both Hughes and Charles were dead to duty, being entirely absorbed in the drama that was going forward under their noses.

"You ought to throw cold water on her," Bella said practically.

She had not joined the others about the settee, but stood beside Jobin, looking, for some odd reason, if anyone had had leisure to notice her, rather overexcited and very much pleased with herself. Mrs. Spear, more at home than any of the rest of

them in the presence of disaster, cast a reproachful glance at her
and said that if Madame would just hand her that glass of brandy
she was sure Lady Thurston would take a tiny sip of it. At the
same moment a loud thunderclap heralded the arrival of the
rain, which descended upon the house with all the enthusiasm of
a spring storm intent upon soaking everything in its path and
rattling all the windows until the house itself seemed to shake.

Lady Thurston, finding herself upstaged by Nature, decided to
accept the brandy from Mrs. Spear, who by dint of a combination of coaxing words and a firm demeanour then succeeded in
wafting the Dowager from the uncomfortable settee into the
morning-parlour, where she installed her upon a sofa and said in
a bracing voice that she was sure she was feeling ever so much
better now.

The Dowager, tearfully accepting a second sip of brandy, said
grudgingly, perhaps just a little, and then looked around at her
diminished audience, for only Sir Mark, Regina, and Wrexam
had accompanied her and Mrs. Spear into the morning-parlour.
Hughes and Charles, coming to a belated sense of their duty,
were occupied in speeding M. Jobin upon his way and Bella, for
unknown reasons of her own, had disappeared upstairs.

"*You*," said the Dowager, fixing her eyes accusingly upon
Regina, "don't understand a mother's feelings—"

"Mama—please!" said Sir Mark, casting an agonised glance
upon Regina and Wrexam.

Regina, who had a fair notion of what was coming, hastily
dismissed Mrs. Spear with thanks, and would have liked to do
the same with Wrexam, but that imperturbable peer showed no
signs of being about to accept his *congé* from anyone. Instead,
he seated himself comfortably in an armchair and, crossing one
leg, impeccably clad in dove-coloured pantaloons, over the other,
observed amiably, "I trust no one will mind if I stay. As a future
member of the family, I naturally feel a certain interest—"

Lady Thurston, ignoring this reference to a mysterious connexion claimed by Lord Wrexam with either her own family or
Regina's, which on ordinary occasions would have aroused her
instant curiosity, regarded him with a severity mingled with the
remains of her recent hysteria.

"I consider that you, Lord Wrexam," she said shrilly, "have taken the most unfair advantage of my trust in you! Did you not promise me to do your utmost to see to it that all thought of this disastrous marriage would be abandoned? And have you done so? Have you?"

"Why, yes," said Wrexam mildly. "As a matter of fact, I have. Ask Mrs. Audwyn if I haven't made a dashed nuisance of myself upon every possible occasion, pointing out to her that she would really be making the most frightful blunder in marrying your son. No offence, of course, Thurston," he added, looking kindly at Sir Mark, "but, really, it won't do, you know."

Sir Mark, pokering up as far as his present embarrassment would allow, began to say that he really could not conceive what business of Lord Wrexam's the matter was, but was at once interrupted by his mama.

"Exactly," she said emphatically, "as I have observed a thousand times, Lord Wrexam! 'It will not do!' I have said to my son. 'You are Thurston of Haddingfield,' I have said, 'and you have certain obligations to your name!' To say nothing of the fact," she went on, looking at Regina with loathing across the storm-darkened room, "that I shall never be able to feel for this young woman, or she for me, the tender sentiments that should exist between mother and daughter—"

"No, no, I should rather think not," Wrexam said, looking from one to the other of them with a judicial air. "Not at all the sort of types to form soul-affinities—"

Sir Mark, however, was no longer listening. Walking up to Regina, who was sitting very erect in an armchair, feeling, as she expressed it later, very much like Mary Queen of Scots as the verdict of execution was being pronounced over her, he said to her in an anguished whisper, "She *would* come, you know. I couldn't stop her. She's been working herself up all day, what with one thing and another, and finally she said wouldn't we at least put off announcing the engagement for a year, and she was coming to appeal to you. And what with the storm coming on and all—she's always been deuced nervous of thunder—by the time we arrived here she was quite out of hand—"

Regina looked up at him and her heart smote her. She saw a

not-quite-young man with an honest, agreeable, and—yes, she was obliged to confess—rather weak face, whom she had allowed to become embroiled in this impossible situation because of a moment's pique against Wrexam. In love with her he well might be, but it was, she was sure, a mild sort of passion from which he must soon recover, and that he would ever be allowed to be happy in marriage with anyone but the kind of milk-and-water miss his domineering mother would choose for him it was impossible for her to believe.

She reached up impulsively and took his hand in hers.

"Dear Mark," she said, "she is right, you know. We shouldn't suit in the least, and I was quite mad ever to let you believe we might. Will you forgive me? It is all my fault."

The words seemed to fall into a sudden silence in the dim room, so that for a few moments the intruding rush of the storm against the windows was loudly audible. Regina, looking up at Sir Mark, saw an indefinable expression upon his face—shock, rebellion, but behind it all surely something like relief? *Good heavens*, she thought with a sudden spirt of amusement, *what a dog's life he must have been leading these past few days! And when a man has passed thirty, surely comfort is as important to him as any woman can be!*

She caught Wrexam's eyes upon her and lifted her chin defiantly.

"Very well, Lord Wrexam!" she said. "You may say, 'I told you so,' if you like. Sir Mark and I have decided that our engagement was a mistake. It is now at an end."

"At an end!" Lady Thurston's ample face, which had been bearing a remarkable resemblance to that of a stout, petulant pug in a temper, suddenly became wreathed in smiles. She pushed aside the vinaigrette which Mrs. Spear had left with her, settled her bonnet at a more seemly angle upon her head, and repeated ecstatically, "At an *end!* Oh, my dear Mrs. Audwyn, I knew from the very start that you were a sensible young woman! Far too sensible, when you had had time to reflect a little, not to see that what you and my poor boy were planning was quite out of the question—"

Sir Mark, who had been looking rather dazed by the sudden

turn of events, at this point said, "But—" in the dogged tone of a man prepared to make objections though hell should gape; but he got no further. In one swift movement Wrexam had risen to his feet and was steering him across the room in the direction of the rain-drenched windows.

"Look here, my dear fellow," he said persuasively, "no wish to interfere, but I strongly recommend you take a look at the consequences before you proceed. Not a word to say against your mother, of course, but when she's on her high ropes matters are apt to get a bit sticky, it appears to me. And she's settled down nicely now—cooing at Mrs. Audwyn like a turtledove. No need to set her off again, don't you agree?"

Sir Mark, casting an uncertain glance at his mother, appeared to consider the matter. But remembrance of the terrors of the scene just past, and the horrid prospect of seeing them instantly repeated were he to persist in his efforts to cause Regina to alter her resolution to write *finis* to their brief engagement, ultimately carried the day for prudence over romance. He said, though in an exceedingly reluctant voice, that perhaps Wrexam was right, and then looked at Regina with the despairing glance of a lover who knows very well that his dream of bliss has been too good to be true.

Meanwhile, Lady Thurston had taken matters into her own hands by rising and saying in brisk tones, entirely belying her former well-paraded state of nerves, that now that everything had been so nicely settled, she would intrude upon Mrs. Audwyn no further.

"I am sure, my dear, that you will find a very good sort of husband one of these days," she said to Regina, with an air of benevolent condescension, "one who is far more suited to your condition in life than My Boy. I have often remarked how very proper it is for widows to marry widowers, and I may say I can think of several gentlemen in that category with quite satisfactory incomes and very nice little properties—"

"Thank you, Lady Thurston, but, really, I should prefer you not to trouble yourself in the matter," Regina said coolly, not knowing whether to be furious with her unwelcome guest or to give way to an almost irresistible impulse to laugh.

Wrexam saw the look in her eyes as Sir Mark escorted his
mother from the room and grinned at her in sympathy.

"Lady Thurston as Cupid—the mind *does* rather boggle at the
idea," he said. "And let this be a lesson to you, my girl, never to
think of marrying a man who is tied to his mother's apron-
strings. Have you *no* sense of self-preservation?"

Regina, who, now that she was safely free of her unwanted engagement, was, with feminine perversity, beginning to feel very
sentimental about her rejected lover, said with a somewhat pen-
sive air that it did not matter about her, but she felt dreadfully
sorry for poor Sir Mark.

"Nonsense!" said Wrexam bracingly. "I should have felt a
great deal sorrier for him if you had gone ahead and married
him"—which seemed to Regina such a decidedly uncomplimen-
tary statement that she was about to take strong exception to it
when the door opened abruptly and Bella walked into the room.

"I saw them go," she announced without preamble, "so I
thought I had best come in and tell you, because even if I did it
behind your backs it was only because I had to. And now I want
you both to know."

Regina and Wrexam, justifiably surprised by this very peculiar
statement, looked at her in some misgiving, and what they saw
did little to reassure them. Bella was standing in the doorway,
rather, it seemed to them, with the air of a heroine of romance
about to sacrifice herself upon the altar of some duty known only
to herself. This sort of thing, Regina and Wrexam both knew,
had been the preamble to so many Stacpoole scenes played out
at a pitch of the highest drama that a premonition of the worst
immediately seized them.

"What—?" they began simultaneously, and then both as simultaneously halted, deferring to the other's right to speak.

"No, *you* go on," Wrexam said to Regina. "What it may be I
have no idea, but I read *Trouble* in the tea-leaves." But Regina,
who felt that, after the scene through which she had just passed,
it was really too much to expect her to face another perhaps
equally unnerving, only looked at him despairingly and remained silent. "Oh, very well!" Wrexam said resignedly. "I'll do
it, then. What is it, you abominable brat?"

"I am *not* an abominable brat!" Bella said indignantly. "It is *you* who have been abominable, Alistair—but I have come to tell you that you will not succeed in your dastardly plans! I daresay you would like nothing better than to ruin Gervais, but it will never happen—not while *I* am here to prevent it!"

Wrexam looked at her in bland surprise.

"My dear good child," he said to her reasonably, "you really must learn to curb this distressing tendency you seem to be developing for taking extraordinary ideas into your head. *What* dastardly plans shan't I succeed in? And why in the name of heaven should I wish to ruin young Lescot?"

"Because you are insanely jealous of him!" Bella said promptly, and with a good deal of relish, it seemed, in spite of her flushed cheeks and indignant air. "You have observed that I—I am attracted to him—"

"Are you, by God!" Wrexam said, and, to Bella's distinct chagrin, a smile of the most unalloyed amusement suddenly appeared upon his face.

"It is nothing to laugh at!" she declared, flinging up her head in what she evidently considered a gesture of challenging defiance. "I am not a child, Alistair, and I tell you—I will confess to you—I love him!"

Regina, during this interchange, had been regarding Wrexam, with a rather odd feeling inside her that if he were to turn pale, smite his brow, or do any of the other rather melodramatic things that gentlemen who have suddenly been crossed in love are popularly supposed to do, she herself would disgrace herself by bursting into tears and running out of the room. She was immensely relieved at this point to see that even this outspoken declaration on Bella's part brought only a look of judicious consideration to his face.

"Well, I daresay you could do worse," he remarked. "He's a handsome cub, of good birth and some fortune, it would appear —but I'm not quite sure, you know, that Arun will like it."

"What Papa thinks," declared Bella largely, "means nothing to me—nothing! My future lies with Gervais!"

"My dear Bella," said Regina, who had recovered herself somewhat by this time, "this is all very sudden, surely! Only this morning you were telling me that you cared nothing at all for Mr. Lescot and intended to marry Lord Wrexam—"

"That," said Bella, casting a glance of ineffable contempt upon Wrexam, "was before I knew the depths to which this—this *creature* could descend in attempting to ruin a man whose only crime has been to engage my affections! When I saw him give to a man he knew to be an imposter the diamonds that rightfully belong to Gervais, rather than have them go to benefit Gervais—"

"You saw that?" Wrexam shook his head reprovingly. "Deuced bad habit to get into, you know, my girl—spying on people when they don't know you're about—"

"Of course you didn't know I was about!" Bella said, with spirit. "You wouldn't have dared to do what you did if you had! And Reggie allowing you to do it, too—!" She looked reproachfully at her cousin. "I shouldn't have believed it of you! But it doesn't signify now, because I have thwarted you!"

"Thwarted us?" Wrexam enquired politely.

"Yes, thwarted you! I have given the diamonds back to Gervais!"—and Bella regarded him triumphantly.

Wrexam looked at Regina, and Regina looked at Wrexam.

"But you couldn't have done that, you know," Wrexam pointed out, after a moment. "I handed them over to Jobin. You can't mean to tell us that *he* gave them to you—"

"*Gave* them to me? No! I stole them!" Bella said, with an even more exalted air of triumph. "I took them out of his pocket while Lady Thurston was creating such a fuss in the hall and he was trying to get his hat from Hughes. He hadn't the *slightest* notion they were gone when he walked out of the house, and I took them upstairs at once and wrapped them up and had Charles take them round to Gervais. So he has them now, and there is nothing in the world that either you or the Comte—I mean M. Jobin—can do about it!"

"Mr. Lescot!" Hughes, with butlerlike propriety, announced at that moment from the doorway.

CHAPTER
17

Mr. Lescot, appearing in the doorway hard on the heels of Hughes's announcement, was seen to be in a state of extreme agitation, as well as rather damp from having braved the furies of the storm, all of which did nothing to detract from the romantic appeal of his appearance. He strode directly into the room, but upon seeing Bella checked.

"Lady Arabella!" he said, in emotion-filled tones.

"Gervais!" uttered Bella, and, running across the room, she flung herself into his arms.

Regina, who had the feeling that events were proceeding at far too rapid a pace for her to keep up with, looked at Wrexam in mute appeal.

"Yes," he said. "It does rather seem as if the fat was nicely in the fire now. I expect we shall have Jobin down upon us at any moment, breathing out fire and slaughter and demanding his diamonds back. I begin to shudder at the thought of the life I should have led if I actually had married that tiresome brat! Would you like me to take this in hand?"

"Yes, *please!*"

Wrexam nodded, and took a step towards the young lovers, which had the effect of causing Bella at once to disengage herself from Lescot's embrace and fling herself, arms dramatically outspread, between him and Wrexam.

"No!" she shrieked. "You shan't!"

"I shan't what, you silly chit?" said Wrexam, looking understandably somewhat exasperated. "If you have the slightest notion that I have lethal intentions towards your young man, you may disabuse yourself of it at once! And go and sit down!" he added, in a voice that made her jump. Lescot endeavoured to say something. "You, too!" Wrexam said. "We have had quite enough of Drury Lane for one day." He looked at Regina. "As a matter of fact, let us all sit down and try to sort out the abominable tangle into which this little nodcock has pitched us—"

"I shall not sit down, my lord!" Lescot announced, standing before Wrexam and looking at him with the sort of proud resolve with which his forebears might have faced the guillotine. "You consider yourself, I have been given to believe, affianced to Lady Arabella—"

"Good God, no!" Wrexam disclaimed hastily. "Nothing of the sort. She's as free as a bird, as far as I'm concerned."

"Well, you *did* want to marry me!" Bella said, looking somewhat incensed by this cavalier denial.

"In one of my less logical moments," Wrexam agreed. "We all have them, I am afraid. Fortunately, I have now recovered from my madness."

"Oh!" said Bella, looking still more incensed. "You *are* the most odious, abominable—!"

"Well, *you* don't want to marry me, so why should you fly up into the boughs because *I* don't want to marry you?" Wrexam demanded. "You aren't being very logical, you know!"

"Logical—no!" Lescot declared, regarding his beloved with glowing dark eyes. "That she is not! But generous, impulsive, adorable—yes!" He turned to Wrexam. "You, my lord," he said, "have never known—you cannot appreciate—what she is. When I think of how she has been sought after, the rank and riches she might have if she chose, and that she has sacrificed all that for *me*—! Up to the time I received the note you sent with the necklace"—this, obviously, was now addressed not to Wrexam but to Bella, to whom he turned once more, irresistibly, as the iron to the lodestone—"I had never dared to imagine, to hope for such devotion—"

"Yes, but she's landed us in the devil's own amount of trouble with all that devotion, you know," Wrexam pointed out. "We'll have the Comte—deuce take it, I *will* keep calling him that!—Jobin down upon us at any moment now, and of course he'll demand the diamonds—"

"But of course he will do so; they are his property," Lescot said. "That is, of course, he *would* have done so, if I had not already sent them back to him—"

"Sent them back to him!" Bella stared at him, aghast. "Sent them back! Oh no, Gervais! And after all the trouble I took to get them for you!"

Lescot took her hand fondly in his. "But no, *ma chère;* do not reproach me," he said. "The diamonds are not mine. You meant well, I am sure, but—"

"But they *are* yours!" Bella wailed. "He's an imposter; he's not the Comte de Chelles at all; *you* are! Oh, Gervais, how could you be so *stupid!*"

She broke off suddenly, and Lescot, too, turned in astonishment to stare at Regina, who had succumbed to helpless laughter.

"*Well!*" said Bella, highly offended. "I *don't* see what you find to laugh about!"

"No, I daresay you don't," Regina agreed, wiping her streaming eyes. "Oh, dear! *Don't* look at me like that, love, or you will send me into whoops again! You see, the thing is, Wrexam has found out that the diamonds are merely paste; in fact, he has actually discovered the jeweller who made them. *That* is why I allowed him to give them to the Comte—I mean, to M. Jobin—because it seemed the best way to get him out of the country without a scandal. And then you ruined everything by filching them from him—only now Mr. Lescot has made everything right again by being so n-noble—"

Her voice wavered perilously on the edge of laughter again. Lescot, who was looking quite stunned, gazed from her to Wrexam with an expression of growing horror upon his face.

"But, good God, do you mean the diamonds I returned to my uncle are *not* diamonds?" he demanded. "Good God! He will think that I—"

"No doubt, being a downy bird himself, he will merely think

you an even downier one when he discovers—one devoutly
hopes, *after* he has left the country—that he has been diddled,
and presumably by you," Wrexam said soothingly. "I really
think, you know, that it is quite time you accepted the fact that
he *is* an imposter. His name is Jobin, and he is your late uncle's
former agent, who found it an easy matter, when the Comte died
during the voyage to America, to filch his papers and belongings
with the connivance of the Comte's valet, who was the only
other person aware of his true identity. I am in the process at the
present moment of tracing the master of the vessel in which the
Comte and his two servants sailed, and he will certainly be able
to confirm beyond the shadow of a legal doubt that it was actually the Comte who died on his ship—"

Mr. Lescot, belatedly obeying Wrexam's order to sit down, at
that moment did so abruptly.

"Good God!" he said again, rather thickly. "If that is so—! By
Jupiter, what a fool I have been!"

"Yes, but it is only because you are too *good* to see how
wicked other people can be," Bella said loyally. "*And*," she went
on, her eyes kindling with indignation once more as she looked
at Wrexam, "I hope you and Reggie realise that it is all very
well, as far as M. Jobin is concerned, to think that *he* has got
only paste jewels for his pains, but the *real* diamonds *should* belong to Gervais now, and so *he* is the one who has been cheated
of them, in the end!"

Regina, to whom this view of the matter had not before presented itself, suddenly lost all inclination to laugh and looked at
Wrexam, appalled.

"Good heavens!" she said faintly. "Does that mean that I, as
Etienne's widow, am responsible—?"

"If you were possessed of ample means," Wrexam replied, "I
should say that you did indeed have a moral responsibility to
make good what young Lescot has lost. As you are not, however,
and there can be no question of a legal responsibility, I should
advise you to put the matter out of your mind—"

"But I *can't!*" Regina said, with growing energy. "It is—it is all
quite dreadful! Poor Mr. Lescot—"

"If it will make you feel any better," Wrexam said soothingly,

"I shall tell you that, as your husband, I shall feel obliged to make a very handsome wedding present to your cousin Arabella when she marries—shall we say, a diamond necklace?—so that Lescot will have no real cause to feel ill-used—"

Regina was staring at him as if she could not believe her ears. "As my—my *husband*—!" she ejaculated incredulously.

"Why, yes," said Wrexam comfortably. "I really think we should be married before this pair of young turtledoves, don't you? After all, we *are* older, and that should give us *some* privileges—"

"But I don't—I can't—you don't—"

"On the contrary," said Wrexam, "I do very much indeed, and I shall be delighted to prove it to you if once we can rid ourselves of these two pestilential children. Isn't there another room in this house where they can carry on their business while we transact our far more important affairs?"

But before Regina could reply, Bella, who had been listening to what had been going on with her eyes as wide as saucers and an expression of rather belligerent incredulity upon her face, said indignantly to Wrexam, "Well! I have never heard of anything more underhanded in my life! Why didn't you *tell* me you were in love with Reggie all the while, instead of making me feel perfectly horrid trying not to fall in love with Gervais, because I thought it would ruin your whole life if I didn't marry you?"

"My dear good child," Wrexam said, amused, "a gentleman can't do the crying off, you know; that is left for the lady. And the very deuce of a time I have had of it, I must say, clinging to the ragged ends of honour while I was longing to tell you to your head that I could imagine no worse fate than being riveted to you!"

"Well, you needn't be insulting," Bella said with some asperity. "But," she added magnanimously, "I do think that you will be far better suited with Reggie, and I am sure I wish you both very happy."

"I," said Regina, rising with dignity at this moment, "shall go upstairs to my room. I have had *quite* enough of having my name bandied about in a matter upon which I have never been consulted in the least—"

"Now do you see what you have done?" Wrexam demanded of Bella. "You have bandied your cousin's name about, and you must have known how much she would dislike that." Bella giggled. "Don't make it worse by laughing, you abominable child," Wrexam admonished her, moving rapidly across the room and interposing himself between Regina and the door just in time to prevent her from leaving the room. "Mrs. Audwyn—Regina— Reggie, my dear and only love—if I promise to consult you until I am blue in the face, will you stay?"

"I cannot go while you are standing in the doorway, my lord," Regina pointed out, thus omitting in the most Machiavellian way to give him a direct answer to his question.

"Then I shall remain here until I am frozen into a pillar of salt, like Lot's wife, or something equally uncomfortable," Wrexam said. "Only I must move far enough to let these two young people out or I shall be obliged to say everything I have to say before an audience—and I *don't* think you would care much for that."

Regina, who was quite sure that she would not care for it at all, gave tacit consent to this manoeuvre by remaining where she was and saying nothing, and Bella and young Lescot thereupon slipped from the room. Wrexam, closing the door behind them, at once said to Regina, in the sudden silence that seemed to fall in the room upon their departure, for even the storm had abated abruptly, "And now, my love—"

"Lord Wrexam," said Regina, who felt that the confusion and flurry into which this totally unexpected turn of events had plunged her placed her at a great disadvantage before his lordship's masterful certainty, "before you go any further, let me tell you that I have never considered marrying for a second time—"

"Well, consider it now," Wrexam urged amiably. "Plenty of advantages to the idea, I should think—especially if one already has a decided preference for the man one is thinking of taking as a husband."

Regina gasped indignantly. "I have never shown you the *slightest* preference, my lord!" she said roundly.

"Oh yes, you have!" Wrexam contradicted her. "Not in words,

no—nor even in actions—but it was in your eyes—" He caught her up suddenly in his arms. "I can't have been mistaken!" he said. "We have both been pitchforked into this by something much stronger than our own intentions, my love, and in spite of our having firmly determined to dislike each other thoroughly! It has been there from the very beginning of our knowing each other, and if that silly little Bella hadn't been standing in our way—"

"That," said Regina, striving most unsuccessfully to maintain an air of aloofness under the twin handicaps of her inability to free herself from his lordship's embrace and the unruly beating of her own heart, "was entirely your own doing, my lord!"

"Exactly! My doing and almost my *un*doing—but fortunately she has fallen in love with someone else, and now there is nothing that stands in our way. *Will* you marry me, Reggie?" He stood gazing down at her, an odd light in his eyes. "You told me once," he said, "that of all the cold-blooded, cynical men you had ever met, I bore off the palm, and that you believed it highly unlikely I had ever formed a *tendre* for any woman. I should like a chance to prove to you now how very much mistaken you were—"

Regina looked up at him. There was nothing, she was obliged to admit, either cold-blooded or cynical in the gaze that was resting upon her at that moment, and she suddenly felt quite certain that if she did not put a stop at once to the scene that was being played out so unexpectedly between them she would find herself in the highly unusual situation of being engaged to marry a man whom she had never until that moment considered in the light of a possible husband.

And was she really in love with him, then? she asked herself in bewilderment. Certainly there was no blind, worshipful infatuation here, as there had been with Etienne Audwyn: she saw Wrexam's imperfections clearly enough. Yet she suddenly felt, with a most unreasonable sort of certainty, that if any single one of those imperfections were to be removed, she would be quite unhappy and even desolate, because Wrexam just as he was—overbearing, acerbic, mocking, opinionated—was exactly the man with whom, for some totally illogical reason, she wished to spend the rest of her life.

"What are you thinking now?" Wrexam demanded. "Good

God, girl, you oughtn't to be thinking anything at all while you are being proposed to and made love to! You ought to be swept along on the high tide of your emotions—"

"But I am! That is exactly what is so amazing!" Regina said, looking up at him with her eyes full of astonishment. "I never thought of marrying you until this moment—and now all at once I know that if I didn't I should never be happy again in my life" —which admission his lordship found so extraordinarily moving and enchanting that he felt obliged to tighten his embrace in a fashion that would have been alarming if it had not been so completely satisfying, and to kiss her in a manner that took her breath away. He behaved, in short, quite as foolishly as young Mr. Lescot was doing, conducting his own equally successful amours with Bella in the back drawing room abovestairs, and forgot entirely his reputation in the *ton* for remaining unruffled in the face of any human experience.

The fact was, his lordship was frank to admit, that he was top-over-tail in love for the first time in his life, and he was so impatient now to assume the rank and privileges of husband that he announced his intention of bearding the first available bishop in his den on the very next day, procuring a special licence, and marrying his true love out of hand.

But to this highhanded procedure Regina, although approving of it thoroughly in principle, was obliged to enter a protest.

"But I can't!" she said. "Not in the middle of the Season! Bella's come-out! The children! We *must* be sensible, Alistair!"

"I have been sensible all my life," said Wrexam, which was a gross exaggeration, for he had not, "and what did it ever do for me but get me next door to engaged to Bella Stacpoole? If Arun has been inconsiderate enough to go off to Mexico, leaving his entire family upon my bride's hands—"

"But he didn't know I was going to be your bride when he went," Regina reminded him. "You wanted to marry Bella then— and I must say," she remarked, not too plainly, for she was now seated beside his lordship upon a gilt pinewood tête-à-tête, and he had taken advantage of the fact that his arm was about her and her head on his shoulder to kiss her in a very ardent manner, "I must say," she repeated, "that it took you long enough to get *un*engaged from her. Sir Mark got unengaged from *me* in no more than four days."

"Yes, but you forget *I* had no mother to help me," Wrexam pointed out virtuously. "If I had, I should have got unengaged like a shot, for from everything I have ever heard of her she was a very strong-minded female, who could have given Lady Thurston cards and spades and still come out ahead in the game. But that isn't the question. The question is, *will* you marry me at once, and let the chips—or the Stacpooles, as it happens to be in this case—fall where they may?"

Regina began to answer him, but was interrupted—perhaps fortunately—before she could do so by a confused noise in the hall outside and the almost immediate entrance of a somewhat agitated Hughes into the room.

"Begging your pardon, ma'am," he proclaimed, with a quite unbutlerlike lack of calm, "but Lord Arun has just arrived—*with* two ladies."

"My uncle? With two ladies?" said Regina. She looked at Wrexam, quite at sea. "But he is in Mexico, or at least on his way there," she protested. "He *can't* be in London! Unless—oh dear, is it Lady Emeline he has brought with him, Hughes? Perhaps something has happened—"

"It is *not* Lady Emeline, ma'am," said Hughes, who had regained something of his customary air of propriety, but still bore in his eyes the eager gleam of a man who, having undergone a shock himself, is eager to pass it on to others. "One of the ladies who is with his lordship is Lady Penfield, with whom I fancy you became acquainted, ma'am, on the occasion of your visits to Ireland. The other"—he paused impressively—"the other," he repeated, "his lordship introduced to me as Lady Arun."

"As *Lady Arun*?"

"Yes, ma'am," said Hughes primly, but looking quite smugly satisfied with the effect his words had produced. "So his lordship said."

Wrexam, seeing that Regina was too stunned to speak, enquired, "Where has his lordship gone now, Hughes? Upstairs to the drawing room?"

"Yes, my lord. I informed him that he would find Lady Arabella there."

"Then I suggest," said Wrexam, turning to Regina, "that we join him there at once. This seems to be a day of surprises, and we had as well find out without delay what Arun has to add to it!"

CHAPTER
18

Lord Arun, when they had walked upstairs, was discovered standing in the middle of the drawing room with his hands behind his back, rocking complacently back and forth from heel to toe and regarding a fascinated audience, seated before him, which consisted of Bella, Lescot, a very pretty, shy-looking young girl in a blue travelling costume and a chip hat, and a good-humoured lady of middle age wearing a Brunswick grey pelisse and a sensible bonnet.

"There y'are, Reggie!" he said with a gratified air as Regina, followed by Wrexam, entered the room. He gave her a peck on the cheek as she automatically approached him, said, "How de do, Wrexam? Not surprised to find *you* here," in an astonishingly friendly fashion to Wrexam, and gestured towards the younger of the two ladies he had brought with him. "Like to make you acquainted with my wife, Lady Arun," he said, with a slight smirk. "Formerly Miss Penfield. Married yesterday in Dublin by special licence. Believe y'already know Lady Penfield. Millie, my love, this is my niece Regina Audwyn—and Lord Wrexam—"

The former Miss Penfield, blushing up to her eyes, murmured a scarcely audible, "How do you do?"—and cast such an appealing glance at Regina that that young lady, making a valiant effort to overcome her astonishment, smiled at her and said with the best approach to pleasant civility that she could muster,

"Well, this is a great surprise! You must know, Miss—Lady Arun—"

"Call her Millie," Lord Arun interjected. "All in the family now, eh?"

"Millie, then," Regina said, smiling again at the shy, newly made countess. "What I had begun to say was that we were quite unaware my uncle was even in England, far less that he had the intention of marrying—"

"Oh, I know what you are thinking, Mrs. Audwyn," Lady Penfield interrupted, speaking in lieu of her daughter, who appeared too much overcome to be able to bear her proper part in the conversation. She was a downright, hearty woman of forty, who, as Regina was aware from her visits to Bellacourt House, was a neighbour of the Stacpooles, a widow known both for her charitable works and for having what many gentlemen who followed the local hunt admiringly characterised as the best pair of hands in the county. "You probably think we have run quite mad —and to tell you the truth, I am not at all sure that we haven't! Here were Millie and I come to Dublin only for a few days' shopping, and went to the play one evening thinking only to amuse ourselves, when who should we run across but Arun? He was on his way to Mexico, as you well know, I daresay, but the weather had other plans, and—to make a long story short, when a three days' gale had blown itself out, he'd already made an offer for Millie and *No* he wouldn't take for an answer, till he brought me around at last to agree to their being wed. Which I couldn't stand out against—not with Millie after me morning and night, too, to give my consent—"

"*Mama!*" said the new young Lady Arun, her face most becomingly suffused with pink colour.

She looked appealingly at her bridegroom, who said to Regina in a complacent tone, "Quite a romance, eh? Love at first glance and all the rest of it. Never thought it'd happen to me. Given me a new outlook on life, y'know. Didn't expect I'd ever marry again. Liked my freedom and all that." He nodded in Wrexam's direction. "Came to me like a flash you had the right idea, after all, Wrexam," he said. "Marry a young wife, just out of the schoolroom, with no fashionable nonsense in her head. Putty in the hands of a man of experience."

And he looked with such an infatuated simper at his young bride that the question as to which of them would be putty in the other's hands was left with no uncertain answer in his hearers' minds.

In view of the alteration that had recently taken place in Wrexam's own ideas on the subject of matrimony, there appeared to his auditors to be no simple and unembarrassing response that they might make to these statements, and a rather delicate pause ensued, which was broken by Lord Arun, who had no delicacy whatever.

"So the thing of it is, Wrexam," he said, with a large air of generosity, "you were right; I was wrong. No objection at all now to your marryin' Bella. Have the wedding next week, eh? No need to put it off any longer; Millie and I want to be off to Mexico."

This time it was obviously imperative for someone to set him right on the drastic changes that had taken place in Wrexam's plans during his absence, and his lordship manfully made an attempt to do so, only to be swept aside by Bella.

"But, Papa, I don't *want* to marry Alistair now, and he doesn't want to marry me!" she said, putting the matter in a nutshell with typical Stacpoole disregard of the need for tact. "I am going to marry Mr. Lescot instead. Oh! You haven't met him, have you? This"—she turned adoring eyes upon the young man beside her— "is Mr. Lescot, only he is really the Comte de Chelles now, because his uncle is dead. But actually it doesn't make a great deal of difference, because people don't have titles in America."

Lord Arun, looking more than a little bewildered and understandably somewhat put out by this sudden flouting of a theory he had evidently come to cherish, said rather peevishly, "I wish you'd talk sense, Bella! Can't make anything out of this rigmarole!"

He regarded Lescot with suspicion. The young man, flushing up to the roots of his hair, said quickly, "I must offer you a thousand apologies, my lord! If I had known you were in the country, of course I should have consulted you before—"

But Lord Arun was not listening. Pointing an accusing finger at Wrexam, he said with extreme severity, "Now see here, Wrexam! If you've been playin' fast and loose with my little Bella—"

"Oh, Papa, for *pity's* sake!" Bella began impatiently.

"If you will allow me—" Wrexam interrupted politely. He addressed Lord Arun. "Bella and I," he said, "have mutually agreed that we are not suited. She has become attached to this very estimable young man, who is by right of birth a nobleman of France and by his own endeavours, I understand, the master of a considerable cotton plantation near New Orleans, in America. I, on the other hand, have formed what I consider a lasting passion for your niece Regina, and we expect to be married at the very earliest opportunity—"

Lord Arun's eyes widened. "What?" he demanded. "What's that you say? You and Reggie—?"

"Exactly," said Wrexam. "You have, I hope, no objections?"

"Objections? Good Lord, no! Told you when you were flourishin' after Bella you'd do better to take Reggie instead. Didn't I? Didn't I?" Lord Arun, flown with the remembrance of his own perspicacity, looked triumphantly about the room. "Remember my very words," he said. " 'If you had any sense in your cockloft,' I said, 'you'd stop tryin' to marry Bella and have a touch at Reggie instead.' And the two of you looked down your noses at me!"

"No doubt we did," Wrexam agreed, with a glinting glance at Regina, "not being gifted with your extraordinary powers of perception."

"Well, I don't say I haven't got 'em," Lord Arun said complacently. "Knew the minute I clapped eyes on Millie, f'r example, that she was the gel for me. Not that I hadn't clapped eyes on her before that, of course. Acquainted with her since she was in short-coats. But this was different. Out of school, hair up and all that. Said that very night to Aurelia—that's Lady P., y'know—that I was goin' to marry her, and, b'God, I did!"

"Well, it will seem very odd," Bella said practically, "to have Millie Penfield for a stepmama, but I expect we shall all grow used to it in the end. And I daresay you will have children of your own in time, Millie, so you won't mind having Giles and Maria to look after, too. Of course Colin is nearly as old as I am, so he needn't signify—"

Lord Arun looked at her a trifle irritably. "Don't keep chatterin' nonsense!" he said. "Of course Millie ain't goin' to look after Giles and Maria. Colin, either. We're goin' on our honeymoon. To Mexico. Probably stay there six months or more. Travel around. Interestin' place, Mexico."

"No doubt you are quite right," Wrexam observed urbanely, "but may I point out to you, Arun, that I, too, have plans for a honeymoon? And I am afraid it would scarcely suit me to be obliged to cool my heels for the better part of a year while you enjoy *yours* before I can be off on *mine*." Seeing that Lord Arun was looking slightly puzzled, he added explanatorily, "You haven't forgotten, I hope, that your children are now left in your niece's charge?"

"Oh—that," Lord Arun said, dismissing the matter easily. "No trouble about that. Lady P.'ll take them in hand. Very fond of children; always has been. Sort of stepgrandmother, eh? Talked it all over beforehand. That's all right."

Regina looked rather doubtfully at Lady Penfield. "But, Lady Penfield, are you sure you don't mind?" she asked.

"Not in the least," said Lady Penfield cheerfully. "I've told Arun, though, that they'll be raised on *my* system, not his, from this time out. Plenty of good food and outdoor exercise, but a proper governess for Maria and good manners from everyone—if that isn't too much to expect from a Stacpoole, which I daresay it is."

Lord Arun, suddenly becoming alarmingly gallant, said that a system that had produced a pearl without price like Millie couldn't be far wrong, and he believed, at any rate, that in studying the culture of the ancient Aztecs he might hit upon some new principle of education that that fellow Rousseau had never thought of. He then expressed a sudden desire to see his other children and herded his bride and Lady Penfield up the stairs to the nursery floor, somewhat in the manner of an overly zealous sheep dog.

"What Colin will say to all this," Bella said, as they departed,

"I cannot imagine. Millie Penfield! Why, we were all used to play together when we were children, and she was the most poor-spirited little thing—!"

"Never mind," said Wrexam. "She obviously adores him, and will follow him devotedly all over the globe, while her mama turns Bellacourt into a haven of good sense and sound living, instead of an elegant madhouse. By the bye, Bella, he hasn't yet given his consent to your marrying your young man, you know."

"Oh, he will!" Bella said confidently. "And if he jibs, there is always Millie. I always could persuade her to do whatever I wished her to, and I am sure Papa will do anything that will please her. But what a very odd marriage it is, to be sure!"

Wrexam said that in his opinion most marriages were, even his own, and, declaring an urgent need to decide immediately upon the date, hour, and place where those nuptials were to take place, carried his bride-to-be off with him again to the morning-parlour, where they fell into an extremely foolish conversation—or at least it would have seemed so to any third person, had there been one present, which fortunately there was not.

At last, however, they recovered sufficient rationality to decide upon being married by special licence in St. George's, Hanover Square, that day week, which his lordship declared to be the outside limit of his patience in the matter, and they were discussing the details of a wedding trip to the Continent when Lord Arun poked his head in at the door.

"*There* y'are," he said, surveying them with an air of satisfaction. "Now, see here, Wrexam, about all these weddings—if you want me to give the bride away, you'll have to make it quick. Say, by next week? I have Bella's set for Tuesday, and I could fit yours in on Wednesday, if you like. Then Lady P. takes the children back to Bellacourt on Thursday and Abby can close the house—"

"Oh!" said Regina, at last able to get a word in. "Then you *have* given your consent to Bella's marrying Mr. Lescot?"

"And why not?" demanded her uncle. "Fine, well-set-up young feller. Knows a good deal about the American Indian. Matter of fact, Millie and I are thinkin' seriously of givin' up Mexico for our weddin' trip and goin' to New Orleans instead.

Lescot's promised to put me in touch with some of the native tribes. Might spend our honeymoon in a tepee—what?" He jabbed a pointing finger at Wrexam. "You and Reggie'd better come, too," he said. "Splendid opportunity to observe the native culture."

Wrexam uncoiled his long figure from the tête-à-tête sofa where he had been sitting with Regina.

"Now, see here, Arun," he said, "you may order the day of my wedding, if Reggie really does want you to give her away, but my honeymoon is my own! And I do *not* propose to spend it in a tepee, along with half the members of my bride's family! Reggie and I are going to the Continent, like civilised newlyweds, far from totem poles and tomahawks!"

"Oh, very well!" said Lord Arun tolerantly. "But you don't know what you're missin', y'know. Amazin' people, these aborigines. Might give you some new ideas. Some of their marriage customs, f'r instance—"

"Thank you, but I believe I shall do very well with the old ones," said Wrexam firmly. "And what, may I ask, does Lady Arun think of this plan of yours?"

"Took to it like a duck to water," said Lord Arun promptly. "Bound to. Likes whatever I tell her she likes." He looked severely at Wrexam. "You had your chance, too, y'know," he said. "Marry 'em out of the schoolroom and educate 'em yourself. As the twig is bent and all that. Works like a charm. Sure you don't want to change your mind and have Bella after all?"

"Your generosity," said Wrexam gravely, "overwhelms me, but, tempting as your offer is, I fear Mrs. Audwyn might not quite like it. You see, I feel she is rather counting upon having me as a husband."

"Mrs. Audwyn," said Regina with mock-indignation, as Lord Arun, nodding indulgently, disappeared as abruptly as he had appeared a few minutes before, "is doing nothing of the kind, my lord! If that is the best reason you can find for marrying me—!"

For answer, his lordship took her with quite uncivil ruthless-

ness into his arms.

"That," he said to her presently, "is my reason," and as the aforesaid Mrs. Audwyn, looking now somewhat dishevelled and entirely blissful, had not a word to say against it, it can only be presumed that she found it entirely satisfactory.